"You were my best friend."

Amy's eyes welled with tears. "I loved you. Cherished you. Thought nothing but the best of you. And then you were gone. You cut me out of your life, and mine became very empty."

Nash shifted in his seat, his face grave.

She shook away the threatening tears, swallowed the lump in her throat. "I didn't know what to do with myself."

He stood, pacing, his movements agitated and robotic. "I hate myself for that."

"I hated you, too." She rose also, rubbing her arms, and gazed at the barn in the distance. Maybe she shouldn't have told him. "I'm not trying to punish you. I just… Well, I needed you to know."

He came up next to her. She dared not move or she'd fall apart. His shoulder was less than an inch from hers.

She squeezed her eyes shut. *Don't remember. Forget it. Forget it all.*

She spun away from him.

"It's your fault, you know. The life I wanted? Gone. You shattered my dreams, Nash Bolton. You shattered them."

Jill Kemerer writes novels with love, humor and faith. Besides spoiling her mini dachshund and keeping up with her busy kids, Jill reads stacks of books, lives for her morning coffee and gushes over fluffy animals. She resides in Ohio with her husband and two children. Jill loves connecting with readers, so please visit her website, jillkemerer.com, or contact her at PO Box 2802, Whitehouse, OH 43571.

Books by Jill Kemerer

Love Inspired

Wyoming Cowboys

The Rancher's Mistletoe Bride
Reunited with the Bull Rider

Small-Town Bachelor
Unexpected Family
Her Small-Town Romance
Yuletide Redemption
Hometown Hero's Redemption

Reunited with the Bull Rider

Jill Kemerer

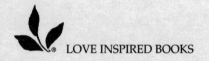 LOVE INSPIRED BOOKS

ISBN-13: 978-1-335-50954-3

Reunited with the Bull Rider

www.Harlequin.com

Printed in U.S.A.

Also I heard the voice of the Lord, saying,
Whom shall I send, and who will go for us?
Then said I, Here am I; send me.
—*Isaiah* 6:8

To my sister, Sarah. You'll always be my hero! And to my brother-in-law, Rich, and my nieces, Eva, Cecilia and Calista. You make life fun!

Chapter One

Tonight was no ordinary night, not for Amy Deerson, at least. She was about to meet the little girl she'd been asked to mentor. When the pastor called yesterday, she'd jumped at the opportunity to spend a few afternoons each week with a neglected child. At four years old, the girl was too young for the church-sponsored mentor program, and the pastor had suggested a private arrangement due to the circumstances. But first, Amy needed to meet the girl's father. He had the ultimate say in whether she spent time with his daughter or not.

Taking a deep breath, Amy got out of the car and approached the church's entrance. It was still chilly for late March in Sweet Dreams, Wyoming, but it wouldn't be long before wildflowers bloomed. Just thinking about flowers, crafts, tea parties and other things small girls enjoyed put a bounce in her step. *Don't get ahead of yourself.* This was the initial meeting. Until the dad agreed, it was not a done deal.

She'd prayed for so long to make a difference in a kid's life, and God had answered.

Amy headed down the staircase to the meeting

rooms. The low hum of male voices quickened her pace. What would the girl look like? Would they hit it off right away? And would the dad be cute?

Cute? Really, Amy? Who cared what the father looked like? A romance would be inappropriate given the situation. And, anyway, she'd been scorched at love twice. She would *not* put her heart on the line again.

The hallway walls were filled with pictures of kids doing crafts at previous vacation Bible schools. Excitement spurred her forward. Life was falling into place. Business was booming at her quilt shop, she'd finally gotten up the nerve to submit a portfolio of her fabric designs to several manufacturers and now this! She'd never intended to remain single, but that's how life had worked out. Helping this little girl would ease the longing in her heart for a child of her own.

She peeked into the preschool room. Hannah Moore, the pastor's wife, was standing next to their toddler son, Daniel, and a young girl.

It's her!

Dark blond hair cascaded over the girl's shoulders. She looked woefully thin under a purple sweater and striped leggings. Amy couldn't see her face, but she stood stiffly near Daniel, who was pushing a toy dump truck on the colorful ABC area rug. As much as Amy longed to join them, she continued toward the door at the end of the hall where Pastor Moore was waiting with the father.

Entering the conference room, she greeted the pastor then turned her attention to the man sitting at the end of the table. Her stomach plunged to her toes, the sensation worse than the roller coaster incident in eighth grade.

No! This can't be... He can't be...

Her knees wobbled to the brink of collapse. Unable to hear a word the pastor was saying, she shook her head, her gaze locked on familiar blue-green eyes. Every instinct screamed for her to run, to get out of there, to make sense of the fact Nash Bolton was in the room.

Nash. The man she'd loved completely. The one she'd thought she'd marry. The guy who had left town over a decade ago—no goodbye, no explanation. The jerk who had never come back.

It hit her then... The little girl she'd been asked to unofficially mentor?

His daughter.

She was having a nightmare. She'd wake up and be in her bed under her favorite quilt—

"Thank you for meeting us tonight," Pastor Moore said.

It wasn't a nightmare. And yet it was.

She blinked a few times and sat in the nearest chair, forcing herself to focus on the pastor's face. In his early thirties, he had a kind air about him.

"Sure." She hoped her lips were curving into what could pass as a smile.

Pastor Moore gestured to Nash. "Amy Deerson, this is—"

"We know each other." Nash's deep voice was firm, and its familiar timbre unlocked memories she'd thought long gone.

She dared not look at him. Couldn't handle whatever she would find in his expression. Regret? Sarcasm? Pity? Didn't matter—her feelings for him *were* dead. She'd been over him for a long time—years and years. The shock of seeing him had sent her into a tizzy. That was all. In a few minutes, she'd be fine.

"Good." The pastor took a seat opposite her. "I've had such a strong feeling about you helping little Ruby."

Ruby. The girl's name was Ruby.

"Amy has been training for several months to be a mentor. She's passed her background checks and is willing to devote the extra time you mentioned Ruby needs. And with none of our other trained mentors available to help at this time, well…it seems ideal. With your permission, I'll tell her about Ruby's situation. Or would you like to?"

Nash brought his fist to his mouth and cleared his throat. He looked older, his face harsher than she remembered. And he'd filled out. Still wiry, but with more muscles in his arms and chest. Gone was the young cowboy she'd loved. In his place was a chiseled man.

Their past flashed back. The day they'd met. Their first kiss. His big grin and slicing sense of humor. The future they'd planned. Oh, how her heart had overflowed for him. And then he'd disappeared, leaving her devastated.

And now he was back. And she—out of all the women in this town—had been asked to spend time with *his child* when all she'd wanted was to marry him and be the mother of his babies? *God, You wouldn't be this cruel. This is a joke, right?*

"Pastor," Nash said, "could you give us a moment, please?"

"Of course." He stood. "I'll see how it's going in the preschool room. Be back in a few minutes."

Amy straightened. She wanted to look away but didn't. It had been ten years. She'd moved on. And the fact he had a daughter made it quite obvious he had, as well.

"I didn't know, Amy. I never would have agreed to come if—"

"If you'd known I was involved." She hated how snippy she sounded. And that his full lips and high cheekbones still made her chest flutter. His cropped brown hair gave him a maturity his previous waves had not. The laugh lines around his eyes were a kick in the gut. He'd been carefree, rising to the top of the professional bull riding circuit while she'd nursed a broken heart. And he hadn't cared one bit.

He hadn't loved her.

He'd loved someone else and had a baby with her.

"So, she's your daughter." She was surprised she wasn't yelling at him.

"No."

No? What was he talking about?

"She's my little sister."

"I know that's not true," she snapped. "You're an orphan."

"Yeah, about being an orphan." He shifted his jaw. "Not quite."

Nash had known moving back to Sweet Dreams was dumber than climbing on the world's meanest bull while recovering from a broken rib, but he'd done both anyway. The bull hadn't been nearly as scary as the thought of running into Amy. He'd been in town a mere week and already his worst fear had come true. Except this was even worse than running into her. This was…horrible… beyond bad.

He'd loved Amy more than anything on earth. That's why he'd had to leave all those years ago—to protect her.

But now another female needed his protection. He

would give Ruby all the love and normalcy he'd missed out on as a kid, and if it meant living in the same town as Amy, so be it.

He just hadn't planned on running into her this soon. In fact, he hadn't put any thought into what he'd do when he eventually *did* run into her, which was inevitable in a small town.

How could he tell her everything that needed to be said in a few minutes? It was hard to concentrate with her big coffee-colored eyes shooting knives his way, not to mention her long dark brown hair tumbling over her shoulders, reminding him of its silkiness. Creamy skin, curvy figure—she looked even better than when he'd left, and she'd been a knockout back then.

"What do you mean, 'not quite'?" Her clipped words told him loud and clear how hard this was for her. He owed her…so much.

"I wasn't an orphan. I lied to you." It had been the only lie he'd told her. And it had torn them apart. She just didn't know it.

"I see."

He hesitated. "The pastor will be back soon, so I'll give you the condensed version. My mother had me when she was fifteen years old. She was a drug addict and, at times, a prostitute. She told me she didn't know who my father was—could have been any number of guys. I haven't seen or talked to her in over ten years. In December I got a call saying she'd died of a heroin overdose. That's when I found out I had a little sister."

The chaos of the past four months gripped his muscles in relentless tension. He shrugged his shoulders one at a time to relieve it, which didn't work. Amy stared at him with a mix of disbelief and disgust.

"How did you get custody of her then? Wouldn't someone close to her, someone she was familiar with, raise her?"

"You'd think so, right?" He flexed his fingers. "Needless to say, my mother didn't leave a will. Ruby's father is like mine—unknown. Our mother was turning tricks for drugs at the time and had no idea who he was. Believe me, the courts and I did our best to find out. We had little to go on. No one else wants the kid."

Amy's face looked ready to crack into a million pieces. "Do *you* want her?"

"Yes."

"A child isn't a duty."

"Exactly." He lightly thumped his knuckles on the table. "That's what I told the judge when I petitioned to be her guardian. I couldn't let her grow up the way I did." He hadn't meant to admit the last part. When they'd dated, he'd purposely not discussed his upbringing with Amy. He hadn't wanted her to know the depravity of his youth. Since he'd moved to Sweet Dreams from Sheridan, Wyoming, when he was thirteen, hiding his childhood hadn't been difficult to do.

What did it matter now? He'd lost all rights with her the day he'd skipped town.

"What do you mean?" she asked.

He had to get back on track. "Ruby's been growing up in a bad—I'm talking highly dysfunctional— environment. The night our mother died, the police went to the apartment she'd been living in. Ruby was there, alone. No food. Heat was turned off. Electricity, too. Who knows how long she'd been there by herself? Believe me when I say the only stable times in the girl's life have been when she was in foster care while our mother was in jail."

Amy's eyes widened, and she blinked rapidly. Then she lifted her chin. "Why here? Why bring her to Sweet Dreams?"

Because he'd had no other choice. Ten years ago he'd purchased a home nearby, but that had been when he'd still believed he could have it all, including Amy.

"I own property outside of town. As soon as the court awarded me custody, Ruby's therapist recommended I get her settled as soon as possible, and she was adamant about Ruby needing stability. I'd bought the house and land before…well…before I left, but I've never lived there. I've been renting it out. The therapist urged me to raise Ruby here permanently."

"Back up." She brought her hand in front of her, palm out, fingers splayed. "You own a house here?"

"Yeah."

"I guess I didn't know you at all." She tucked her lips under as if trying to get her emotions under control. "Not an orphan. Bought a house—I'm assuming when we were still together. What else didn't you tell me?"

Regret thundered through his veins. He wished he was on a bull, in the chute, ready to be released into the dirt arena. It was the only place he'd ever been able to escape. He imagined wrapping his hand with the rosined rope…

"Never mind. I don't want to know." She turned her head to the side, exposing the pale skin of her neck.

"The reason I left—"

"No." She held her hand out. "You don't get to do this now. I'm not interested in your confession. It's too late. I'm here for one reason—to mentor a little girl.

Whatever you want to get off your chest will have to stay there."

"You would still help her?" Nash had to give it to her—she was courageous. He'd always admired her quiet strength, her morals, the way she'd soothe anything bothering him. And he'd thrown it all away.

"I don't know." Her dark eyebrows formed a V. "It's a lot to take in."

"She's withdrawn, malnourished, fearful. She was placed with a young couple while the courts decided if I could be her permanent legal guardian. I visited as often as allowed. It took a long time before she warmed up to me. The day I gained custody was the day we moved here. The therapist thought it would be best. No more temporary living arrangements."

"So you're here to stay."

"Yes."

"For as long as Ruby needs."

"Forever. Dottie Lavert will help out when she can. Clint's nearby. Wade isn't far. Marshall, too." Clint Romine, Wade Croft and Marshall Graham were his best friends—practically his brothers—from his time at Yearling Group Home. They'd all been sent to the group foster home as young teens, and they'd stayed friends as adults.

"Good. Sounds like you don't need me."

"I wouldn't be here if Ruby didn't need someone. The therapist wants her to have a positive female influence. A consistent presence—someone who can give her a better understanding of how a caring woman acts. Basically, the opposite of our mother. It's too much to ask of you, though. Like I said, I never in a million years would have dreamed…"

"What? That I would want to help a child?"

That you wouldn't have a houseful of kids of your own. And he knew she didn't. Clint had told him she was single. He had no clue why. She was the most nurturing person he knew.

"Clint told me you keep busy with your quilts and the store. I didn't think you'd be willing to give up so much time for a stranger's kid."

"Yes, well, I like children, and I want to make a difference. I just think the situation is too bizarre for me to be Ruby's mentor. It would be uncomfortable for us both."

Exactly. This had been an extremely uncomfortable ten minutes.

"I agree. Hopefully, the pastor has someone else who can help. I'm not looking for a babysitter—I retired from bull riding and I'll be spending all my time with Ruby until she starts school next year—but given the circumstances…well…she needs more than me."

Amy wrapped her arms around her waist and didn't reply.

The problems he'd faced over the past four months galloped back. Learning his mother was dead. Retiring from the profession he'd loved. Figuring out how to live in one spot when all he'd done was travel for a decade. Raising Ruby, who was emotionally stunted, when he had no idea how to be a parent. And this meeting— he'd been so hopeful the woman would be exactly what Ruby needed. From what the pastor said, no one else was available. A clawing feeling gripped his throat.

He wasn't equipped for any of this. And he really hated failing.

"I hope you were able to catch up." The pastor

walked back in, a big smile on his face. "Amy, now that you are more aware of what Ruby has been through, do you have any questions? Concerns?"

"Yes."

The hair on the back of Nash's neck bristled.

"As Nash mentioned, we knew each other a long time ago. In fact, we dated. Given this information, don't you think someone else should be paired with Ruby?"

"Well, it depends." He cupped his chin, rubbing his jaw. "I'm assuming it wasn't an amicable parting."

Amy quickly shook her head. Nash looked away.

"If you both can put your personal feelings aside and keep Ruby the main priority, then I don't think there's a problem. But if there is any revenge in either of your hearts, I urge you to decline. You won't be able to support Ruby the way that she needs. We must all work together for her. She's been through enough. Wouldn't you agree?"

"Yes," they replied at the same time.

"Since you dated some years ago, I'm guessing you've both moved on, so I don't think it will be an issue. And it's up to you two how much interaction you want to have. Amy, why don't you meet Ruby before making any decisions?" The pastor tilted his head, watching her response. She considered for a moment before nodding. He smiled. "Good. I'll take you down there. Nash, you wait here, and we can talk more when I get back."

Nash tracked Amy's moves as she left the room. An ache spread across his chest. She would never agree to help Ruby.

Lord, I can't do this alone. Please have mercy on me.

He'd given Ruby a nice house, clothes, food and love,

but he couldn't give her a mother. The only woman he'd ever wanted was Amy, and he'd never forgive himself for leaving her in such a cowardly fashion. He hadn't given her a warning, hadn't even said goodbye.

Moving back to Sweet Dreams and glimpsing Amy occasionally would have been punishment enough, but being in regular contact with her?

He couldn't imagine a more painful scenario.

She'd been his. And he'd forfeited all claims to her.

He should be glad Amy wouldn't agree to this arrangement. Would make life easier for him. But where did that leave Ruby? He could not let his baby sister—the child he now considered his daughter—to grow up as damaged as him.

"You must be Ruby." Amy crouched in front of the play kitchen where the tiny blonde stood. The girl flinched, backing up to the wall. Amy ached to put her at ease. "I'm Amy."

Ruby's mouth slackened, her blue-green eyes opening wide with distrust. Nash's eyes. She resembled him in other ways, too. Wide forehead, high cheekbones. But Nash's nose was longer, while Ruby's was a perfect button.

Hannah and little Daniel were coloring pictures at one of the children's tables. Amy wasn't sure what to do. The girl's body language shouted fear.

"Would you like me to read you a book?" Amy gestured to the beanbags next to a small bookshelf.

Ruby didn't blink, didn't move. Her lips trembled.

"It's okay." She longed to touch her cheek, to reassure her, but she sensed any physical contact would terrify the girl. "Why don't I pick one out, and you can come over if you'd like?"

She crossed to the shelf and selected a Curious George picture book. Then she lowered her body into one of the beanbags. How she would get out of it, she had no idea. Boy, it was low to the ground. Ruby hadn't moved but still stared intently at her. Amy plastered on a big smile and waved for her to come over.

Ruby didn't so much as twitch.

Maybe if she started reading it, the girl would join her. She read the first five pages out loud and peeked over the cover. Still staring. She read five more pages. Ruby had drifted a few feet in her direction. Progress. She continued until the end. Ruby stood about three feet away, her eyes locked on Amy's face.

"You know, pretty soon you'll be able to go to school, and you'll learn how to read."

"I know some letters." She spoke with a lisp.

Amy nodded, encouraging the sign of interest. What this child must have been through. Left unsupervised with no food or heat. Disgraceful.

"Do you see any letters you recognize on the cover?" Amy held the book out.

"*E. O.*" She pointed to the letters.

"Good job! You're very smart. Do you want me to read another book?"

She didn't respond.

"Why don't I pick one out?"

Pastor Moore and Nash came into the room. Ruby raced to Nash, wrapping her arms around his legs as if she never wanted to let him go. The sight made Amy's stomach clench. Ruby trusted Nash. It was obvious.

And if Amy had to guess, the child didn't trust another living soul.

"Hey, RuRu, how do you like this fun place? We'll be coming to church here every Sunday." He hoisted her into his arms, settling her on his hip. She let her head fall onto his shoulder and wound her arms around his neck. "Us grown-ups have to talk a few more minutes, so you stay here and color with Daniel, okay?"

She buried her face in his shoulder.

"Honey, I will only be gone a few minutes." His voice was soft, tender. He glanced at Pastor Moore, then Amy. "Would you give us a sec?"

"Of course." The pastor waited for Amy to join him, and they went back to the conference room. "What did you think?"

"I think you were right to contact me. I know it's not the church's traditional program, but she seems... well...a bit traumatized."

"Yes. She's been through a lot. Tell me, Amy, do you see yourself as being her mentor? Now that you know her situation? Not to mention the man who will be raising her is someone from your past?"

Ruby's face, demeanor and adorable lisp all came to mind. Yes, she could see herself as the girl's mentor. She longed to make life better—normal—for the sweet child. To earn Ruby's trust would mean the world to her.

But interacting with Nash?

No.

Just no.

Sure, she'd moved on and didn't need to know Nash's reasons for leaving, but the hurt was still there. Even if she and Ruby only met privately, looking in the girl's eyes would be like looking into Nash's. Amy didn't know if she could do it.

But how could she admit to the pastor all the thoughts churning in her brain?

"I have a lot of mixed emotions about this. If it was anyone but Nash, I'd be setting up a schedule tonight. She's so teeny. And four years is a dear age."

"Are you over him?" the pastor asked gently.

"Yes." She nodded too quickly. "Haven't seen him in a decade."

"I see. Are you worried you won't be able to handle a long-term commitment with Ruby?"

Was she? Any arrangement with Ruby meant interacting with Nash. What if she got mad at him, or he blurted out the reason he left and it devastated her? Would she still be able to give Ruby the attention she needed?

"Kind of. This is all sudden."

"Let's pray about it." He bowed his head, and Amy clasped her hands. "Heavenly Father, You are all-knowing and almighty. Please give Amy and Nash clarity about what is best for Ruby. If Amy isn't the person You have in mind to help, make that clear, and lead another of our church members to step forward and answer the call. Above all, we pray You will heal Ruby's hurts and comfort her. Lead us to support Nash as he navigates the new waters of fatherhood. In Your name we pray."

"Amen," Amy whispered. The reference to answering the call pierced her conscience. It had been more than a year since she'd begun praying about mentoring a child. How many times had she prayed to be paired with a young boy or girl? Too many to count.

"If you're willing, let's ask Nash and Ruby to meet us here again tomorrow night. It will allow you to spend a little more time with her before making your decision. If you want to help, you and Nash can work out a schedule then. If not, I'll talk to him about other options."

"I think that's a good idea. Are there any other mentors who could help Ruby?"

"Not at this time, but a few of our retired ladies might be willing to spend a Saturday afternoon each month with her."

Amy frowned. Would a few Saturday afternoons be enough for Ruby?

Nash came back into the room. His Western shirt and jeans couldn't hide the fact he was built out of rock-solid muscle. It wasn't as though she was attracted to him—she merely had eyes. He was a good-looking man. Who'd broken her heart and left her so he could ride bulls and be a superstar.

"Ah, Nash, good. Amy and I were talking about not rushing into this. Would you be willing to come back tomorrow night? Given this new development, I think you both could use some space before making a decision."

"Sure." He crossed his arms, then quickly uncrossed them. "And if it's a no?"

Pastor Moore smiled. "We have options. None as good as Amy, but don't worry. We won't let you and Ruby down."

"Okay. Does seven work for you?"

Amy nodded. Why was she even considering this setup? No one—*no one*—would fault her for saying no. If it was anyone else, she'd do it. She ignored the voice in her head telling her she was only thinking of herself. Maybe she was, but who could blame her?

After murmuring goodbye, she hurried out of the room and stopped in her tracks. Ruby stood with Hannah and Daniel in the hallway. Her blank expression turned Amy's legs to lead.

If only the child would smile or cry or…something. Amy had been around a lot of children during her years teaching Sunday school. She was used to the highs and lows of their moods. However, she couldn't categorize Ruby's emotional state. She seemed completely unengaged with the world. No joy, no hope—nothing.

As much as Amy wanted to avoid Nash, she also wanted to brighten this little girl's life. Give her a reason to smile.

She had a lot to pray about.

"Guess what?" She approached Ruby, bending to speak at her level. "We can read another story tomorrow night. How does that sound?"

Ruby looked at her blankly. "I like the monkey book."

"I do, too." Amy straightened, surprised at the emotion clogging her throat. "See you tomorrow."

If she agreed to this, she'd lose her heart to Ruby. Maybe already had. Losing her heart to a child she could handle. But losing it to Nash again? She would never let that happen. Not when her life was finally falling into place.

Chapter Two

Nash clipped the walkie-talkie to his belt and strode to the barn the next afternoon. Breathing in the cool air, he let the sun's rays soothe his agitation. Ruby had fallen asleep watching cartoons. Normally, the girl didn't nap—she fought sleep something fierce—so the fact she'd conked out was a blessing. He'd only been her guardian for a week, and already the role felt impossible.

He wasn't a dad. He was a broken-down, retired bull rider. Sure, he'd risen to the top of his profession and made gobs of money, but he didn't know how to do domestic. At thirty-one years old, he had a lot of life left to figure out, like how he was going to spend his days from now on. Inspecting his property would be a start.

Snow must have thawed recently for the ground to still be soft. This part of Wyoming tended to be dry. He checked the walkie-talkie again. If Ruby woke up and he wasn't there... Her terrified face from two nights ago still bothered him. He'd put her to bed, read her a story and gotten ready to leave. She'd clung to his arm, shaking her head, her eyes wild. He'd asked her what was wrong, but she just kept repeating, "Don't go." So he'd stayed until she fell asleep. An hour later, she'd woken up, screaming. Scared him half to death. He'd cradled her in his arms, wishing he could have been there for her from birth to protect her. It had taken another hour before she'd stopped shaking.

Sometimes he wished his mother was alive just so he could chew her out. But she wasn't, and he was left to fix her mistakes. Not that Ruby was a mistake...but her upbringing had been disastrous.

Could he fix Ruby?

Yesterday he'd bought the walkie-talkies and showed Ruby how to use them. He'd said, "If I'm not in the room with you, all you have to do is press this button and holler for me. Then take your finger off, and you'll be able to hear me talk." They'd practiced until she was an old pro.

He chuckled. He'd probably be at her beck and call from now on. Not that he minded. The girl was as cute as could be. His mission was to help her find her smile. He wanted to keep it there. Make her forget a lifetime of trauma and neglect.

He slid open the barn door and counted the stalls as he walked through. Enough for ten horses. He already owned six. His friend Wade had been boarding them for him while he was on the road competing. The other outbuildings held his equipment. The property had one fenced-in pasture and plenty of land for any number of operations.

Lately, he'd been thinking about opening a training facility for young bull riders. But he wasn't sure if he should. Just because he had the property to train kids didn't mean he had the ability to teach. Maybe he'd be better off breeding horses. He certainly wasn't running a cow-calf operation like their friend Clint. Which reminded him…he hadn't talked to Marshall in a while. He'd better call him soon.

After shutting the barn door, Nash went back into the house. A pang of regret hit him every time he entered. Before moving back, the last time he'd been inside had been the day he'd bought it as a surprise for Amy. An engagement present. He'd been planning on proposing to her the next week. Then his mother, once again, had destroyed his life.

The diamond ring still sat in its box in his top drawer. He really should sell it.

Like he ever would.

He checked on Ruby, asleep and curled up in a tight ball like a dog afraid of getting kicked. He kissed her soft cheek before going to the kitchen. The company he'd hired to paint and decorate the house had done a good job. He'd given them free rein and a blank check. Just told them to make it feel like a family lived there and to make sure Ruby's room was fit for a princess. If only money could fix all of his problems, but the millions in the bank couldn't win Ruby's trust or buy Amy's forgiveness.

Amy was going to say no to helping Ruby. And while her refusal would be best for him, it definitely was not best for Ruby.

The girl hid apples and packages of crackers under her pillow and in her closet. He'd found cookies in her shoe. The therapist had warned him it might take a while for her to believe she'd always have enough to eat. Whenever he found food, he was supposed to gently remind her she was safe with him and he would always provide for her.

He sat on one of the bar stools at the island, dropping his forehead into his hands. The enormity of the situation threatened to overcome him.

I'm not qualified for this. What if she always hoards food and wakes up screaming? What if she never smiles? Is too scared to go to school? What if she's been damaged beyond repair?

He raised his head toward the ceiling.

God, I need You.

Ruby had no one but him.

He'd handle it. He had to.

Amy girded her shoulders and entered the church at 6:55 pm. She'd spent the past twenty-four hours talking to her mom, her best friend, Lexi Romine, and the Lord. Lexi and Mom thought she should decline being Ruby's mentor. The Lord, it seemed, had other plans.

Every time she prayed, she kept coming back to Isaiah 6:8: "Also I heard the voice of the Lord, saying, Whom shall I send, and who will go for us? Then said I, Here am I; send me." She'd prayed for so long to help a child. How many times had she thought *Here am I, Lord. Send me*?

And now that the opportunity was here, she couldn't justify turning it down. Every time she tried, her argument fell flat. She kept thinking of the Old Testament story about Joseph. If Joseph could forgive his brothers for selling him into slavery and then provide for them so their families didn't starve, couldn't she move past her issues with Nash to help Ruby?

Maybe this was her cross to bear.

But could she bear it?

With her back straight and head high, she strode to the preschool room. This wasn't for Nash. It was for Ruby.

Maybe Nash didn't keep his promises, but she kept hers. She'd promised the Lord she would do His will.

She believed this was His will.

After entering the room, she halted at the sight of Ruby on Nash's lap. The child held a stuffed sheep in the air and was pretending to make it dance. She wasn't smiling, but the fact she was playing was a good sign.

"Hello, Ruby." She waved. "Who is this sheep? He's quite the dancer."

She immediately clutched the animal to her tummy like a wild rabbit stilling at the first hint of danger.

Nash took the sheep out of Ruby's hand. "I think this is Sheldon. Sheldon the sheep. Is that right, RuRu?"

She turned to see his face. A hint of a smile lifted her lips, and she nodded.

"Or it could be Samantha." Amy slowly approached them, trying to be as non-threatening as possible. "Are you sure it's a boy?"

He flipped the sheep over twice then sniffed its head. "It smells like a boy. It's not all flowery like a girl." He held it up for Ruby to smell. She took a sniff. "What do you think?"

"Boy," she said.

"Well, it is very nice to meet you, Sheldon." Amy held her hand out and pretended to shake the animal's paw. "Would he like to sit on your lap while we read a book?"

Ruby didn't respond.

"Should we try another Curious George? See what trouble that silly monkey gets into today?"

Amy selected a book and folded her long legs to sit in the beanbag, grunting as she sank the final inches. Ruby brought the stuffed animal over. She didn't sit, though.

"Stay?" Ruby asked Nash, her gaze full of worry.

"I'd hate to miss the story." He folded his legs to sit cross-legged on the carpet. The process looked painful. Ruby, clutching Sheldon, settled on his lap, and he tickled her side.

"Daddy!" She giggled and squirmed. Nash stopped teasing her, kissing the top of her head instead.

Daddy? Amy ignored the pitter-patter of her heart at the sight of Nash in such a paternal role. Maybe if she and Ruby met privately, the arrangement would work. They could make cookies and color. They could go to the library and check out books or stop into The Beanery for hot chocolates.

If she was going to be part of Ruby's life, it had to be on her terms. And that meant spending time alone with Ruby. No Nash allowed.

After reading two books, she asked Ruby if she wanted to pretend to bake a cake. Ruby followed her to the play kitchen, and Nash declared he'd be back in a few minutes. He had to speak to the pastor. As soon as Nash left, Ruby became expressionless, the way she'd been in the hallway yesterday.

"First we need flour and sugar." Amy pointed to the fake boxes of food. "Can you find them?"

She stood with her arms glued to her sides. *Okay.* Amy grabbed a box and pretended to pour it into a plastic bowl. "Mmm... I love cake batter. Here's some butter. Throw it in." She handed plastic butter to Ruby, who let it fall into the bowl.

"And eggs. My cakes always have eggs. Let's crack them." Amy tapped the plastic egg against the table and pretended to drop it in. Ruby ignored the egg in front of her. "We're ready to mix." She found the plastic hand-mixer and gave it to the girl. "Give it a good stir."

She obeyed, but Amy got the impression she was merely going through the motions, that she wasn't enjoying herself.

Hannah and Daniel entered. "Hello, you two. Ruby, would you mind staying here with Daniel and me while Amy talks to your dad for a minute?"

Ruby just stared at her.

"I won't be long." Amy found Sheldon and gave him to Ruby. "Here. Make sure this sheep doesn't get into any trouble." Although she hated leaving her, she went to the meeting room.

"Well, I trust you've both had time to pray about the situation." Pastor Moore waited for her to sit. Nash was in the same spot as yesterday. "What do you think?"

She considered for a moment. The previous twenty minutes solidified her opinion. With patience and a woman's touch, Ruby had a better chance at coming out of her shell. And Amy wanted to be that woman.

"I would like to spend more time with Ruby." Amy watched Nash. He jerked to attention. "But I don't know if you'll be comfortable with my suggestion."

His eyes darkened. "What is it?"

"Would you be okay with me spending time with Ruby alone? I'd love to show her around my studio, take her to the library, that sort of thing."

He bowed his head. "I'm not sure."

"I don't know if I can agree if it's going to be the three of us all the time. It's a bit intimate given our history."

He blew out a breath. "I understand. Really, I do. I'm thinking about Ruby. I know you'd be good for her, and frankly, I'd prefer she spend time alone with you. But she's going through a lot. What do you think, Pastor?"

He'd prefer not to be around her, either? Why the words hurt, she didn't know. It's not as if the past ten years hadn't proven the fact.

"I think you should follow your instincts, Nash." The pastor addressed Amy. "Ruby is afraid of strangers. It will take time for her to get used to you. She might need Nash with her until she's comfortable."

Amy swallowed the sour taste in her mouth. It wasn't as if she didn't know the pastor had a point, but she was already going out on a limb by agreeing to this. Couldn't they cut her a break?

"I guess we could do a trial run," she said. "Say, a few afternoons next week and see how it goes? If we aren't feeling it, we'll go our separate ways."

"Works for me," Nash said gruffly.

Pastor Moore stood. "I'm here if either of you need to talk or have additional concerns. Feel free to call. Why don't I let you two work out the details of next week?" He left the room, and the air felt charged as soon as he was gone.

With no idea what to say, she fixed her gaze on the map of ancient Israel hanging on the wall. Nash remained silent, as well.

"How weird is this for you?" Amy finally asked him.

"Really weird." His throat worked.

"Gives me a new appreciation for what divorced

parents must go through. Coming up with a visitation schedule, figuring out drop-offs and all that."

"Except we were never divorced," he said. "Or married."

The words hurt, she couldn't deny it, but Nash seemed unsure of himself, and Amy had never seen this side of him. He'd always been quick with a joke and oh, so confident.

He massaged the back of his neck. "Sorry... Thank you for agreeing to help Ruby. I know you don't want details, but what I did back then was unforgivable. I at least want you to know I hated leaving you."

Then why did you?

She didn't want to know.

"It was a long time ago." She waved the apology off like a pesky fly. "Which days work best for you?"

Storm clouds brewed in his eyes, but he accepted the change in subject. "Any you have free. I have nothing going on."

"So you really retired?"

"I did."

She wanted to ask what he planned to do next, but she stopped herself. She didn't need personal information from him. She'd stick to business—to Ruby. Which reminded her...a few things had been niggling in her mind.

"Does Ruby know you aren't her father?"

"Yes. I explained I'm her much bigger brother. It took several supervised visits at her foster home before she'd even speak to me."

"But she calls you Daddy."

He shrugged, a smile briefly lighting his face. "When I told her she was going to live with me, I asked her what she wanted to call me. She said, 'How long am I going to live with you?' I told her forever. She replied, 'Daddy.' I tell you, my heart melted into a puddle right there on the linoleum floor of the courthouse."

Amy's heart was growing squishy, too, and that wouldn't do. *Remember the days after he left? How you sat by the phone hoping he'd call? And don't forget how awful it was to read about him winning the event in Houston. Going on with his life as if you'd never meant a thing to him.*

"Yes, well, that's good." She reached into her purse for her planner. Opening it, she scanned the next week's schedule. "Why don't we do Tuesday and Thursday, say, three o'clock? You can bring her to my apartment. It's above Amy's Quilt Shop. Just go around the back and up the stairs. I have a studio I think she'll enjoy."

All the brightly colored fabrics, the work tables, sewing machines and art supplies were sure to please the girl. She'd plan a few simple crafts for them to do.

"You don't have to work at three?" He frowned.

"No, I hired a high school girl to work afternoons."

"Tuesday and Thursday then. Listen, Ruby is shy around…well, everyone. She might have a hard time being in a strange place without me."

"You could go to The Beanery after you drop her off. If she gets upset, we'll join you and get a hot cocoa or something."

"That might work." His face cleared, and his shoulders relaxed. "Does this mean you'll make a final decision next week?"

"Do you really want me to spend time with Ruby? Or do you feel cornered into it?"

"I want Ruby to trust other people. I mean, she'll be

going to school soon, and I don't want her scared of her teachers. Would it be easier on me if someone else was her mentor? Yeah. But I'm grateful you're willing to try. She needs more than I alone can give her."

So having a different mentor would be easier on him, huh? She bit back a nasty retort. The insecurity in his eyes pacified her irritation. Her decision wasn't about Nash anyway. It was about trusting God even when the circumstances didn't make sense. She'd always wondered if she would step up and take care of an enemy if put into the position of being a Good Samaritan.

She'd regret it if she didn't at least *try* to help Ruby.

"Then, yes, let's see how the visits go, and I'll give you a firm answer next week."

"Wade's delivering my horses soon." Nash sat in a white rocking chair on his front porch Tuesday afternoon. Clint Romine, one of his best friends, sat next to him in an identical chair. Ruby was picking pasqueflowers from the yard. He still had a little time before he had to take her to Amy's place. He had no idea how their meeting would go, but he feared the worst. Those early visits with her at the foster home had been terrible. But maybe Ruby was in a better mental place now. He hoped so.

"How long has it been since you've ridden Crank?"

"Four months. I'm itching to saddle up. Could ride for days, I think, and I'd still feel as restless as a mountain lion."

"You've been traveling the circuit since we graduated high school. Of course you're restless." Clint lived outside of Sweet Dreams with his pretty new bride, Lexi, who happened to be Amy's best friend. Another complication Nash didn't know how to handle. Would his move back to Sweet Dreams be awkward for Clint and Lexi, given how he'd treated Amy years ago? He'd worry about it another day.

Nash sighed. "I've got to figure out what I'm going to do now that I'm here."

Clint stared ahead, slowly rocking. How could he sit there so calmly? Nash was about to bust out of his rocker. He didn't care if the decorator claimed the chairs cozied up the porch; they made him feel like a grandpa. A sprint up the drive would go a long way to helping him let off some steam. But the sad truth was he couldn't sprint if he tried. His body had been so beaten up and battered that he had trouble even jogging.

"Thinking about ranching?" Clint asked.

"No."

"Breeding horses? Wade could help with that."

"Maybe." He stood and paced the porch, his movements choppy. "I've been thinking about something different. I'm not sure it would work."

"What's that?"

He stopped at the column nearest Clint and leaned against the railing. "I might open a training facility. For young bull riders."

Clint considered it a moment. "I could see it."

"But I don't have the experience to teach kids."

"What are you talking about?" Clint laughed. "You have more experience in your pinky finger than anyone I know."

"Yeah, but that's riding bulls. Not *teaching* kids to ride them."

"You'd be great. What would you need?"

"Steers. Bulls. A practice arena. Chutes. Equipment. Insurance—a lot of insurance."

"There you go."

"But knowing what I've been through, do I want to encourage kids to follow in my footsteps? You know the injuries I've sustained. And I was fortunate."

"It's a dilemma, that's for sure. I guess you'll have to pray on it."

Last year, Clint's response about praying on it would have annoyed Nash. But after he'd had a string of bad rides and broken his ankle and ribs for the umpteenth time, he'd spent a few months at Wade's secluded ranch—a thirty-minute drive from Sweet Dreams—and gotten right with his Maker. He prayed about everything now.

"Will you pray about it, too, brother?" Nash asked.

"Of course." Clint rose, nodding toward Ruby. "How's she doing?"

"Better than I expected. When I first met her, she was so skinny her bones pushed against her skin. She was terrified. Skittish." He shivered thinking about her back then. "I'm really sorry I missed your wedding, man. I never would have—"

"Don't say a word, Nash." Clint shook his head. "I understand. I would have been furious if you'd have come to the wedding when you found out about Ruby. She needed you."

Ruby approached, eyeing Clint with distrust and avoiding him. She thrust a bouquet of purple blooms in Nash's hands.

"For me? Well, RuRu, these are the purdiest flowers I've ever seen. Thank you kindly." He winked at her. "And don't worry about Clint here. He's one of my best buds. We lived together when we were teens. You'll meet my other friends, Wade and Marshall, soon enough."

Ruby hid behind his leg. He knew her well enough to assume her gaze was fixed on Clint.

"I've got to be going." Clint tipped his Stetson to Ruby. "Good to meet you. Maybe your dad will bring you out to the ranch sometime. We have lots of horses and cows and dogs. You like dogs?"

No answer. Thankfully, Clint didn't seem to need one.

"Thanks for coming." Nash clapped him on the back. "Don't be a stranger."

"Bye." Clint waved and ambled to his truck.

"Well, what do you say we get these in some water before we head over to Miss Amy's?" Her eyes had questions—a lot of questions—but he couldn't read her mind. "What's wrong? You're worried about something. I can tell."

He opened the door for her, and they went to the kitchen, putting the flowers in a mason jar with water.

"You a little scared of her?" He boosted her to sit on the counter.

"No."

"What is it? You can tell me anything."

"How long do I have to stay?"

He smiled at her lisp whenever she said her *s*'s.

"You don't have to stay at all. But if you want to, you'll be there for one hour. And I'll be three stores down, slurping coffee. You and Amy can join me if you want, but I'd like for you to give her place a try without me first."

She gulped, her eyes wide and fearful. "One hour? How much is that?"

He almost laughed. He'd forgotten that little kids didn't have a strong sense of time. He pointed to his watch. "When this small hand goes all the way around once, an hour has passed. Maybe you need a watch of your own. We can order one for you. But right now, we've got to skedaddle if we want to be on time."

He picked her up, grabbed his keys and carried her to the garage. After strapping her into her car seat, he backed out and drove toward town. Despite the assurances he'd given Ruby, he had a bad feeling about this visit. Ruby already seemed fearful. What if she made a scene at Amy's? If she did, he wouldn't be able to leave her there, and then Amy would back out.

If Ruby was upset about staying with Amy, he wouldn't force the issue. The kid had been through enough. He just hoped his uneasiness didn't mean his fears were about to come true.

Chapter Three

Amy hummed as she fluffed the throw pillows on her couch. Ruby would be here any minute. She rushed to the other side of the open living space where she kept her private sewing and art studio. If she wasn't cutting material, quilting or making patterns for her weekly blog, she was drawing designs for her own fabric line. Well, hopefully, her own fabric line. She should be hearing back from the fabric manufacturers within a few weeks. How many years had she dreamed of stocking the designs she'd drawn? She shook her head. None of that mattered right now. Her sole goal today was to make Ruby comfortable.

A knock on the door made her pause. *Lord, please give me the wisdom to help her.* She'd show Nash his fears about leaving Ruby were off base. She'd been around young children her entire life. She knew what little girls enjoyed. It would just take a while for Ruby to get used to her. No big deal.

She opened the door. Nash held Ruby in his arms. *Oh, my.* He looked every bit the cowboy she remembered in his hat, jeans, jacket and boots.

"Come in. I'm so glad to see you again, Ruby. Let me take your sweatshirt." She waited while Nash helped Ruby out of her pink hoodie. "I'll show you around my place."

After hanging the hoodie on a hook near the door, Amy veered left to the open studio. She stopped next to the floor-to-ceiling shelves, which held fabrics in a rainbow of colors. In the center of the space, Ruby clutched Nash's hand.

"You did all this?" Nash let out a low whistle. "Everything is so organized. You actually make all those quilts you sell?"

"Most of them. I consign a few local artists' quilts, too." She shouldn't be so pleased at his reaction. He seemed to fill the room with his charismatic energy. He used to draw her like iron to a magnet. She gestured to the rack holding her latest creation. "I'm trying a new pattern."

He and Ruby inspected the rust, cream and navy design. "Patriotic. I like it. Reminds me of the Fourth of July."

"I'm hoping to finish it in June. Red, white and blue quilts always sell well in the summer."

"Speaking of this time of year…" He looked down at Ruby. "Pretty soon you and I will be watching rodeos on Friday nights. Sounds fun, huh?"

Her eyes gleamed almost aqua as she nodded up at him. The sight touched Amy.

"I can't wait for cotton candy and barbecues." He rubbed his stomach. "Mmm-mmm. Makes me hungry just thinking about it. In fact, I'd better get something in my tummy before it growls and scares the neighbors. I'll be heading over to The Beanery. Text me if you need me."

He kissed the top of Ruby's head. Then he nodded to Amy. "I'll be back in an hour. You girls have fun."

As soon as the door clicked behind him, Amy let out a sigh of relief. She couldn't help it. The room felt more spacious, less combustible without him there. She brought her palms together and turned her attention to Ruby.

"I have a ton of markers. Why don't we color?"

Ruby gazed intently at the door, her face white as a fresh snowfall.

"He'll be back before you know it." Amy tried to re-assure her by gently taking her hand, but Ruby yanked it out of her grasp. Her lips trembled, grew blue around the edges. Tremors shook her shoulders. The poor thing was petrified!

Amy knelt beside her. "Ruby, what's wrong? It's okay. You're safe with me."

Her eyes were so wide, so fixed on the door. Amy clearly wasn't getting through to her. What should she do? The way Ruby had flinched at her touch, Amy didn't want to scare her further, but she had to divert her attention away from the door.

Why was she so upset? Nash told her he'd be back in an hour. The child knew he was going down the street to the coffee shop.

Amy stood up, raising her face to the ceiling. *What now?* Whatever was going through Ruby's mind was so frightening, she couldn't move.

"Honey, why don't we go get a hot chocolate with your dad?"

Ruby blinked, shivering. Then she looked away from the door at Amy. Tears began to drip from her eyes to her cheeks. She didn't say anything. Simply nodded.

Amy tried not to let her disappointment show as she helped Ruby into her hoodie. Whatever had happened to this girl in the past had clearly traumatized her. Nash had mentioned neglect and malnourishment, and Amy had brushed over those words as if they hadn't mattered. She should have paid more attention. She'd been so caught up in her own past she hadn't asked the necessary questions.

The psychological damage must have cut deep. Was Amy qualified for this?

She led Ruby to the staircase. "Hold my hand, okay?"

Ruby tucked her tiny hand in Amy's. The gesture pinched her heart. If only she *could* help this girl. She needed more information. And that meant, as much as she didn't want to, she'd have to find a way to meet privately with Nash.

The coffee was perfect—strong with a kick to it. Same as he liked his bulls. He grinned at his own inside joke. The Beanery was quiet. He hadn't been in here before. Looked new, rustic. Smelled great, too. He took a drink. Leaving Ruby hadn't been too bad. She hadn't thrown a fit or anything. So why couldn't he dismiss the nagging worry in his brain?

He smacked his forehead. He hadn't stopped to ask Ruby if she wanted to stay. He'd just left.

He should have asked her. Why hadn't he thought to ask her? His knee was bouncing triple time. *Get yourself together, man.*

He checked his watch. He'd been gone seven minutes. Fifty-three minutes to go. It was times like these that made him wish he was a reader. A book would help pass the time.

The door clanged open, and Ruby raced to him, her face beaming. A lead weight dropped in his gut. If they were here and it had only been seven minutes, the visit couldn't have gone well.

He swung her onto his lap and gave her a big smile. She didn't need to know his emotions were churning. "To what do I owe this pleasure? I thought I was picking you up in an hour." He noted the tear stains down her cheeks and fought back a groan. "You were worried I'd be lonely, weren't you? That's awfully nice of you to be thinking of me."

She rested her cheek against his chest, and he brushed her hair from her face, holding her tightly. Amy stood behind the chair across the table. He mouthed, "What happened?"

She shook her head quickly and mouthed, "Later."

"Can I get you a hot chocolate, Ruby?" Amy asked. "With whipped cream?"

Ruby nodded. If she wasn't so fragile, he'd remind her of her manners. But right now *please* and *thank you* were the least of his worries. If he couldn't leave her with Amy for ten minutes, would he ever be able to leave her anywhere?

A vision came to mind of kindergarten in another year, and instead of Ruby waving happily as she walked into school with a backpack and a lunchbox, he saw her trembling, crying, unable to enter. Some of the bull riders' wives homeschooled their little ones. Would he be forced to do the same?

Homeschooling?

Him?

The coffee threatened to come up. He didn't think he had it in him to homeschool. Maybe he should call the therapist.

"Here you go." Amy beamed at Ruby as she set the cup

down. Nash could see the worry in her exquisite brown eyes. And he recognized her tic from all those years ago—she rubbed her index finger and thumb together whenever she was out of her element. For a second he felt sorry for her. Wanted to make it better, like old times.

Old times. The best days of his life. Even better than winning his first Professional Bull Riders World Championship at the age of twenty-three. Every minute with Amy had been like a dream.

Ruby reached for the cup and licked the whipped cream.

Amy smiled, scrunching her nose at the girl. He had to avert his gaze at all the affection in her expression. He used to be the recipient of it. The past ten years suddenly felt bleaker than he remembered them.

"I was wondering," Amy said, tracing the rim of her mug, "would you two mind if I came over later? I've never seen your house." She gave Nash a charged look, and he instantly understood. They needed to talk but not with Ruby around. And the only place they could reasonably expect privacy was in Ruby's domain.

"Sure." He knew she was going to back out of their arrangement, and he didn't blame her. He suppressed a sigh. "How about seven-thirty?"

"Great." She sipped her cocoa. "How is it, Ruby? Chocolaty enough?"

"Mmm." She sat on his lap, happily slurping her cocoa. He had to hand it to the kid—she bounced back quickly. His spirits sank, realizing how much hope he'd put into Ruby spending time with a woman. Would take some of the pressure off him. Not to mention, he hadn't had more than a minute to himself while Ruby was awake since the day he took custody. If she couldn't handle being with someone as nice as Amy for short periods, what chance did he have at giving her a normal childhood?

Amy began talking about the daily coffee flavors, and they chatted about other changes in the town. Anyone who walked by would think they were having a pleasant visit. A couple of old friends catching up. And he was glad she could be civil, even if they'd never be friends.

By the time they'd all finished their drinks, he didn't know what to do. He hadn't begged for anything since he was a small boy, but thinking about Ruby's future made him desperate enough to contemplate begging Amy to reconsider.

He just wished he had another choice.

"She's out."

Amy waited for Nash to join her at his kitchen island. She'd arrived an hour ago, and she'd tried to engage Ruby by asking her about the toys in the living room, but Ruby hadn't seemed interested in them. Only when Nash had suggested watching a Disney movie had Ruby's face lit up. Thankfully, she'd fallen asleep halfway through *Frozen*. Not that Amy had anything against that particular cartoon; it was just hard to be in a family-type environment with Nash, especially given what she needed to ask him.

She needed the full story of Ruby's past.

Her mind had been so preoccupied, she hadn't had time to truly process his gorgeous house or the fact it was exactly the type of home she used to dream about, back when she still had hopes of getting married and having kids of her own. She'd thought she'd be raising a family in a place like this with property not too far from town. She'd thought wrong.

"Are you sure she won't wake up?" She didn't want Ruby to stumble in on them discussing her.

"I don't think she will. She woke up briefly when I pulled the bedspread over her, but I stayed until she fell asleep again."

One look at his face and all the questions she'd rehearsed earlier vanished. His eyes always changed to gray when he turned melancholy. Seeing the slate shade brought a ping of sadness to her heart. She'd always done her best to soothe his blue moods. But that was then and a lot of life had happened since he'd left. He would have to deal with his moods himself.

"I take it she fell apart when I left her at your apartment earlier."

"I wouldn't say she fell apart." Sitting on a stool, she folded her hands on the counter. "It was actually worse than falling apart. I don't know how to describe it except she almost seemed catatonic. It scared me. I didn't know what to do. She was terrified. Couldn't stop staring at the door after you left. Her face turned white. She trembled. When I suggested meeting you at the coffee shop, she finally snapped out of it."

He frowned. "What did she do then?"

"Tears started falling, but she listened to me and held my hand all the way to The Beanery."

He drummed his fingers on the counter. "Makes sense in a way."

"It doesn't to me, and that's why I'm here." She raised her chin. "I need to know more about her childhood."

Fear flashed in his eyes.

"I need to know it all." Amy wasn't backing down

on this. Either she had all the facts to come up with a realistic way forward to spend time with Ruby, or she had to walk away.

"You're not going to like it."

"I'm well aware of that."

"This needs to stay confidential. I want her to have no baggage in this town. I don't care who knows I'm really her brother raising her as my daughter, but no one needs to know the horror this kid's been through."

"Agreed. You have my word I will not tell anyone the details you share."

"I've told you about our mother." He crossed his arms over his chest, leaning forward. "She went through cycles of heavy drug use and court-mandated rehab. When she was using, she'd do anything—and I mean anything—to get money for her fix. Prostitution. Theft. You name it. She had no sense of time, no sense of reality. Since Ruby had no father or siblings living with her, the poor kid had to rely on herself when our mother was higher than a kite. Inevitably, our mother would get picked up by the cops and thrown in jail for whatever she was guilty of, and while she served time, Ruby would be placed in foster care. But our mother would get out and she'd be clean, so she'd get custody again until the cycle repeated."

"How often did this happen?" Amy's mind was spinning from the scenario. She pictured Ruby small, hungry, scared. She also pictured an unstable drug addict not taking care of the girl.

"Too often."

What did that mean? Every two months? Once a year? She sighed. It didn't really matter. "So walk me through the things she had to endure."

"Being left alone in a filthy apartment with limited food. Could have been a couple hours. Sometimes, I'm sure it was days."

"Days? But she was practically a baby!" Amy brought her hand to her chest. *Horrible.* "She needed a babysitter. No young child should be left alone in a house for any length of time."

"Trust me. I know." He exhaled loudly. "Then there was the fact our mother used around her. Ruby grew up around drug paraphernalia. I guarantee Ruby witnessed her shooting up. I'm sure there was emotional abuse, as well."

Tears threatened at the thought of sweet Ruby going through all that.

"And this went on her entire life?" Amy sniffed.

"Yes. Up until mid-December at least."

"If her case workers knew all this, why did they ever let her return to her mother?" The injustice of it made her want to wring someone's neck.

"They want to keep families together, and they didn't know all of it."

If they hadn't known all of it, and he hadn't seen his mother in a decade… "How do *you* know this is what happened?"

He bowed his head briefly before meeting her eyes. "From experience."

It took a few seconds to register, but when it did… She shook her head slightly, her gaze still locked with his. "I see."

And she did. These new facts sliced open her heart. She'd thought she'd known Nash when they'd dated. She'd always sensed the pain under his easy smile. Understood there were things so awful from his past he might not ever be able to share them. But she hadn't known this.

"You could have told me," she said softly. "You know, back then."

He looked away.

Apparently, he disagreed. She straightened, forcing herself to get her head back to the here and now, not stuck in the way back when.

"Now that I know more about her past, I think she's terrified of you leaving her." The more Amy thought about it, the more obvious it became. "She is much more comfortable with me when you're in the room. But the instant you left today—well, I think she has no idea if she'll be left by herself, dragged to another home or if she'll ever see you again. How long have you had custody?"

"A little over a week. But I've spent time with her almost every day since December."

Amy sagged on the stool. She hadn't realized… No wonder Ruby was so scared. Amy never should have pushed for her own agenda, having Ruby come to her apartment without Nash.

"Well, spending time alone isn't going to work until it sinks in you will always come back for her."

"You're right." He stretched his head back. "Listen, there are a few other things you should know."

She braced herself.

"Since she never knew when she'd have food, she hoards it. I find all kinds of snacks in her bedroom. Sometimes under her pillow or stuck in a shoe. And if she wakes up and I'm not around, she screams. Loud. I bought walkie-talkies so I can go outside if she naps, which she doesn't do very often."

"That breaks my heart."

"Mine, too." He tapped the table, raw honesty pouring from his expression. Then he pointed to the living room. "I bought her all those toys, but she won't play with them. Barely looks at them."

"I noticed the same earlier."

"The therapist told me this is common in severely neglected kids."

"Will she overcome any of this?" Amy held her breath. *Please let him say yes.*

"Most likely. If she feels secure. That's why I moved back. Called the pastor when Dottie told me about the mentor program."

Something in his tone, the dip of his shoulder, clued her into something she'd missed since seeing him again. He didn't want to be back here. He never would have stepped foot in Sweet Dreams again if it hadn't been for Ruby.

Because of me. Because I'm here.

Her heart hurt all over again. Ten years and the wound hadn't fully healed.

"All these questions... Does this mean you still want to help her?" The question came unexpectedly, and Amy almost jumped.

Knowing what Nash had told her, did she still want to help Ruby?

Yes!

The intensity of the thought surprised her. But she had to protect her heart where Nash was concerned. She couldn't trust him with it. She might not even be able to trust herself with it. She was willing to take that chance if it meant bringing sunshine to the little girl who'd only known darkness.

"I want to help her. But I think we're expecting too much of her too soon."

"What do you suggest?" His eyebrows drew together, and he clasped his hands tightly.

"In the pastor's office, we all agreed that Ruby's needs come first, right?"

"Yes," he practically growled.

"Then you and I are going to have to put aside our issues to let her get used to me."

"I'm not following."

"The three of us are going to have to spend time together if Ruby's ever going to trust me enough to be alone with me."

He looked nauseous. Irritation flared in her chest. *Welcome to the club, buddy. It isn't easy for me to be around you, either.*

"You'd really do that…given what I put you through?"

She gave him a firm nod. "Yes. But we need to make it crystal clear to Ruby we are only friends, and there will never, ever be anything romantic between us. I don't want her to be confused about my role in her life."

"Of course. Never, ever will there be anything romantic between us."

"Then we agree." She should be thankful. But his *never, ever* had been more forceful than hers.

"Agreed." He rounded the island and stuck out his hand. She placed hers into it, and his rough, warm skin caused the hair on her arms to rise. He smelled familiar, like aftershave and leather. She snatched her hand back.

Never, ever.

Wouldn't be difficult as far as she was concerned.

"For how long?" he asked.

"For as long as it takes."

Chapter Four

"I'm going to soak up a few rays while you create your masterpieces. I'll be sitting out here if you need me." Nash slid open the patio door while Amy and Ruby dipped paintbrushes into a cup of water. Once he closed the door and sat in a wrought iron chair, he glanced through the glass at Ruby. Her paintbrush was raised and her eyes locked on him. He waved. She didn't wave back, just resumed sloshing her paintbrush on the paper. A good sign.

The cool wind whooshed under his collar. He welcomed it. Being cooped up indoors had never been his style, and hovering in the kitchen for the previous hour, trying not to notice Amy, had ramped up his nerves. He was still attracted to her. Maybe even more than before. When they'd dated, he'd been young and brash and out to prove something, and now…well, he had nothing left to prove. He'd thought being the best bull rider in the world would wipe away his childhood, make him feel like *somebody*. But rather than giving him an identity, all those championships had merely hammered home the fact he was alone. No loved one to celebrate with.

No wife to shower with his financial blessings. As a result, he'd taken more and more risks. And grown hollow inside.

Having Amy around reminded him of the emptiness all too well.

He'd forgotten her rich laugh, the way she always smelled like she'd just baked cookies, the sweet way she had with people. Her patience with Ruby had nearly choked him up earlier. He hadn't realized how overwhelmed he'd felt since finding out Ruby existed. Only two days had passed since Amy had agreed to mentor Ruby. Once the painting session ended, they would talk to Ruby about Amy's role in her life. They'd keep it simple.

Although every cell in his body wanted to stand, to pace, to *do something*, he forced himself to sit there for Ruby's sake. He'd remain where she could see him. Didn't want her thinking he'd abandoned her or something. Amy's insight about Ruby being afraid he'd leave made sense. Growing up, how many times had he felt the same?

But sitting still was hard. He longed to check the stalls in the horse barn again. Nothing but the best for his horses. They'd be arriving tomorrow. Most of them were retired rodeo horses he'd purchased over the years from washed-up cowboys no longer able to support noncompeting animals. Nash had been paying Wade to pasture them. In a way, Wade had pastured him, too. For the past decade, one of Wade's empty guest cottages had been where Nash crashed when not touring. Wade owned a lot of prime land in Wyoming and oversaw a lucrative horse breeding business as well as a cow-calf operation. Wade's employees took good care of Nash's horses, and he never worried about them, knowing they were living the good life.

Yesterday he'd organized the tack room, supervised the hay delivery and checked the pasture and fences with Ruby by his side. She liked the outdoors. Acted more like a normal kid outside than in. He'd been the same way.

The sliding door opened, and Amy poked her head out. "We're done. Come and see Ruby's picture."

He pushed himself to stand, wincing as his hips adjusted. His injuries had all healed, but most days his body felt like it belonged to an older person, not to a man in his prime.

"Let's see what you made, RuRu." He stopped behind her chair, and she looked over her shoulder at him, hope and fear in her expression. He recognized it well. As a kid, he'd never known when his mother would scream at him for no reason. Living with her had been tumultuous in every way. That's why he'd been so grateful for Hank, the man who'd introduced him to bull riding. As a kid, Nash had spent his summers traveling to rodeos with the cowboy who'd briefly dated his mother.

"It's a bunny," she whispered as her slender shoulders slumped. He frowned. Did she think he'd make fun of her or something?

"I love how you made the bunny blue and purple." He knelt beside her, kissing her forehead. "You did a bee-yoo-tiful job."

Her shining eyes met his, and she wrapped her arms around his neck so tightly he almost choked.

"This painting is a keeper." He patted her on the back. "We're going to have to figure out a place to hang it."

"Thanks, Daddy."

Amy had been cleaning the supplies. She packed everything into a large quilted tote bag.

"You know who else we need to thank?" He tweaked her nose. "Miss Amy. She's a good art teacher, don't you think?"

Ruby's face fell, but she nodded once.

"Do you want me to say thanks with you?" He kept his arm around her waist.

"Yes."

"Okay. Ready?" He held his finger up. "Thank you, Miss Amy."

"Thank you, Miss Amy," Ruby mimicked politely.

"You are very welcome, Ruby." Amy smiled. "I enjoyed painting with you. In fact, I have lots of fun projects for us to do together."

She gave him a pointed look. That was his cue. Time to talk to Ruby about her. He'd keep it simple, the way Amy asked, but his memories and regrets warred in his mind.

"Here. Have a seat, Amy." He pulled a chair out for her, and they all sat around the kitchen table. Nash turned to Ruby. "I know this has been a lot of new stuff for you, RuRu. Now that we're settled in here, I want you to have some girl-time now and then. Don't want you stuck inside with an ornery old cowboy like me every second. Miss Amy would like to spend more time with you."

"Don't you want me anymore, Daddy?" Ruby's stricken face was like a kick to the ribs.

Nash inwardly groaned. *God, why didn't I anticipate this? I'm clueless at this dad stuff.*

"Of course I want you, Ruby. Why would you think

I don't?" He plucked her out of her seat and set her on his lap. "I'm your daddy. Forever. Remember? You will always live with me. I will always want you."

"And I don't have to live at Miss Amy's?" Her forehead was creased with worry.

"No! Is that what you thought? No, Ruby. Amy is our friend, and she knows you've been through some rough patches and wants to make life a little happier for you. That's all."

Amy reached over to place her hand on Ruby's. "Your daddy is right. I'm not here to take you away. You'll always live with him. At church I signed up to hang out with a little boy or girl, and the pastor thought I'd enjoy spending a few afternoons with you each week. Your dad and I are old friends—just friends. I'm here for you, not for your dad."

As if he needed to be reminded.

He tried to appear upbeat. "What Miss Amy is trying to say is she's not my girlfriend or anything."

"When I said I'm here for you, Ruby, I meant it. And it's just a few times a week. Do you have any questions?"

Ruby looked like she had plenty but was too scared to ask them.

"Well, if you think of any, you can always ask me. We can talk about anything you'd like. I'm a good listener." Amy stood, picking up her tote bag and waving at Ruby. "And now I'd better get out of your hair. See you soon, Ruby."

"I'll walk you out." Nash followed her to the front door, pausing on the porch. "What's next?"

"That's up to you."

Her fresh-baked cookie smell hit him full force,

made him want to lean in and touch her hair. He backed up a step. "Next week, Tuesday again?"

She shook her head, her pretty brown eyes intense. "I would like to see Ruby more frequently until she's comfortable with me. I'm worried too much time between visits won't serve her well. What about Saturday? The three of us could have lunch at Dottie's Diner or something."

"Good idea. Dottie's Diner. Saturday." He tried to pretend he was pleased for Ruby's sake, but the ping of hope in his chest wasn't about Ruby. He liked being around Amy. And though they would never be a couple again, he didn't mind hovering around the edges of her warmth.

He just had to be smart enough to douse any fantasies of a future with her. They didn't have one, and he'd best not forget it.

"You'll have to bring her to the Easter egg hunt," Amy's mother said. "It's a week from Saturday. Mark it on your calendar."

Her mother, Ginger Deerson, was practical. Outspoken, but practical. And Amy needed a dose of honesty right now. Because watching Nash interact with Ruby had thawed a tiny patch of her heart. What if that spot spread through the whole thing? It would be a disaster.

"I'll mention it, Mom." Amy sipped hot tea in her parents' living room. She'd driven there after leaving Nash's. The one-story brick house looked the same as it had her entire life, and it always comforted her. A safe place in a stormy world. Being around Nash was throwing her emotions into hurricane conditions.

"I finally heard from your brother. He thinks he'll be home later this summer."

"Really?" It had been months since she'd seen Matt. Older than her by two years, Matt was currently on a sea tour as an officer of the navy. "Did he say when?"

"You know him. Can never get a straight answer. At least you fill me in on your life." Mom clicked a pen and jotted notes on her ever-present scratch pad. "I'm not a hundred percent sold on you being around that bull rider so much, but we'll make sure Ruby melds right in with the Sweet Dreams community. Does she like animals?"

"Animals? I think so." Amy let the part about "that bull rider" slide. Mom had never liked Nash. Thought he was too wild for her. She'd wanted Amy to find someone dependable, someone who held a steady job with benefits. Well, a few years ago Amy had found Mr. Dependable, and she'd fared no better with John Mc-Cloud than she had with Nash. Both men had seemed on the verge of proposing. Both men had skipped town.

She still didn't know why they'd left her behind.

Mom rapidly clicked the pen a few times, which meant she was scheming. Her short brown hair had been curled and locked into place with super-hold spray. "Dooley Hill found a batch of kittens in the barn. He's trying to find them all homes. Maybe Ruby would like one."

"Maybe. I don't know." Her mother was the activity director at Sweet Dreams Senior Center. She knew everyone's business, including Amy's. Meddling aside, Amy loved her. Without her parents' love and emotional support, she didn't know what she would do. "It's not really my place to get her a kitten."

Her mother waved, scoffing. "You're doing the man

an enormous favor after the way he treated you. It certainly *is* your place. Find out what color kitten she wants, and I'll have Dooley set one aside. They're still too young to leave their mama, but they'll be weaned in a month or so. I'm pretty sure he said they were tiger-striped or black, but he might have a calico in the bunch, too. I'll ask." She grabbed her cell phone and texted Dooley, an eighty-year-old regular at the senior center.

"Dooley texts?" Amy's mind was officially blown.

"Well, of course he does." Mom's tone was incredulous. "Who doesn't?"

"Clearly I'm out of touch. But back to Ruby…she might not be ready for a cat."

Mom pulled her are-you-crazy face. "What is there to be ready for? It's a kitten. Little girls love kittens. Remember Renaldo? You dressed that butterball up and pushed him around in your plastic shopping cart for hours. The two of you had more fun together."

Renaldo had been an extremely obliging feline. Amy had loved that cat. Maybe she should take one of Dooley's kittens for herself.

And maybe she was avoiding the real reason she was here.

"Mom, I have a question for you, and I need you to take about thirty seconds and really consider it before answering."

"Thirty seconds?" She scowled. "What is that supposed to mean?"

"Just that you tend to toss out answers first and reflect on what you said later." She didn't want to offend her mother, but…

"You got me." Mom laughed, setting the pen and her phone on the arm of the chair. Her oversize navy

T-shirt hung loosely, hiding the evidence of her love of desserts, which Amy had unfortunately inherited. "Go ahead. Shoot."

Was this wise? Asking her very biased mother for her opinion? She decided to go for it.

"Why do you think Nash left?"

Mom opened her mouth to reply, then closed it. After a few seconds ticked by, she folded her hands in her lap. "I think he was selfish. Maybe he thought you would hold him back. Or he might have met another girl on the road. You always had morals, and I think they made you attractive to him, but they also could have pushed him away. Who knows? Maybe he liked the limelight, wanted to be a big star."

Hearing her mother's opinion was hard, but it wasn't anything she hadn't told herself many times.

"Why?" Mom studied her. "Don't tell me he wants to get back together with you."

"No." She shook her head. "Seeing him again dredged up all these things I've pushed away for a long time. Like how he left. And then John…"

"John was a coward, Amy. I never would have encouraged you to date him if I'd known he was going to quit his job and move away with no warning. You wouldn't have been happy with him."

"I don't know about that. He was a nice man. I don't think I would have been miserable, but you're probably right. I wouldn't have been very happy either." It had been a few years since she'd dated John, and Amy didn't miss him one bit.

"Did he ever give you any explanation?" Mom had badgered her about John for months after he left, but Amy had been so hurt and embarrassed, she'd refused to say anything. Eventually her mother had stopped asking.

"Yes." She remembered every word John had said that night. "Sweet Dreams stifled him. He didn't want to be a bank manager."

"Well, what *did* he want to be?" She might as well have said, "Who does he think he is?"

"I have no idea. He said he was crashing with a friend in Miami until he figured it out. He mentioned running a fishing charter in the Keys."

"And that was it?"

"Yep."

"A fishing charter. John? I'm not seeing it. Had he ever been on a boat?"

Amy shrugged. "I don't know. Doesn't really matter."

"Do you miss him?" Mom reached for her pen again.

"No."

"And Nash?" The pen clicked.

"It's been ten years, Mom. We're not getting back together. In fact, we told Ruby we're friends and there isn't anything romantic between us."

"Good. Don't want that little one confused. Losing her mama must have been difficult enough. I don't want you confused either."

"That makes two of us." She hadn't told her mother all the details about Ruby, only what Nash had approved.

Mom's phone dinged. "Oh, good. Dooley says he has three tigers, one black-and-white kitten and no calicos. Too bad. Little girls tend to love those calicos. Are you staying for dinner?"

"Sure. Want me to help?" They rose and went to the kitchen.

"Why don't you chop the lettuce for a salad? Oh, and Amy?"

"Yeah?" She opened the fridge, glancing back at her mother.

"Be careful. You have a big heart, and I don't want to see it broken."

Amy found the lettuce. At least she and her mom agreed on something. She had no intention of letting her heart be broken. She'd be careful, just like her mother advised.

"Whew! That went smoothly." Nash wiped his forehead and set his hat back on his head. "Thanks for coming to help."

Clint, Wade and Marshall stood along the fence, watching the horses get used to their new pasture. Nash had visited them at Wade's whenever he could. And now they would be here full time. He was looking forward to caring for them.

Horses, his buddies and rodeos had always made sense to him. Women? Not so much.

"I see Crank is as rowdy as ever." Clint, tall with dark brown hair and piercing blue eyes, watched Crank prancing along the fence line. "He's showing off for Dixie."

"He's always showing off for Dixie." Nash chuckled. Crank was his go-to horse, his favorite, the one he rode as much as possible. Dixie and Crank, still in their prime, were the youngest of his horses, and they were the only ones he rode. The other four were enjoying their twilight years being pampered.

"I've never seen a horse so similar to its owner." Wade's blond hair was streaked from the sun, and his blue eyes were set in a permanent squint. Made him look like he was always smiling. Wade shook his head. "What a showboat."

"Showboat? Me? No way. I'm a serious, respectable gentleman."

"Gentleman?" Marshall let out a guffaw. "If you're a gentleman, then I'm a royal prince."

"You wound me, Marshall." Nash pretended to clasp his heart. "I hold doors open for ladies and say please and thank you and all that."

"Speaking of ladies…" Wade had his innocent look on, but it wasn't fooling Nash one bit. He was going to ask about Amy, but Nash wasn't talking about her. Period. Wade grinned. "You and Amy were quite the pair back in the day. How are things between you now?"

Nash gave Wade the stink eye then turned to Marshall, the easiest going of the bunch. "So you're really working for your sister's husband? I thought you weren't keen on cowboying anymore."

Marshall's face fell. He and Marshall were about the same height, but Marshall had always been stockier. Pure muscle. His dark hair and scruff gave him a rugged air. "Belle needs me. Now that she's pregnant, she's scared. I don't mind."

"But I thought you liked working for the Beatty Brothers." Clint, usually quiet, shifted to face Marshall. "You've got serious skills fixing big machinery. You sure you can't just visit Belle now and then?"

"No. I told her I'd be there for her, and I'll be there for her." Marshall's tone left no room for arguments. Nash had never fully understood Marshall's devotion to his twin sister, Belle, but lately it made sense. He'd be there for Ruby, too, no matter what.

They let the subject drop. Wade addressed Clint. "It's nice to see you again. You finally broke away from the bride. How is life at Rock Step Ranch?"

Clint colored. "Perfect. Twister's going to be a fine herding dog."

"The honeymoon must be over if you're talking about a border collie and not Lexi," Wade teased.

"Lexi's great. I still can't believe we're married. She's planning about a bajillion weddings here in town. She's happy, which makes me happy." Clint looked around. "Hey, where's Ruby?"

Nash had been keeping an eye on her and pointed a few feet away where she sat cross-legged in the grass, watching the horses as if she couldn't get enough of them. He'd introduced her to his friends earlier, and she'd sat on the picnic table, watching them unload horses and get everything settled in the barn. She hadn't made a peep.

"I've got a good little helper here." Nash was surprised at the emotion welling up within him. Her tiny fingers were picking apart a blade of grass, and her long hair played in the breeze. He loved that girl. "Feeding and mucking stalls will be much easier with Ruby helping."

She glanced up at him with shining eyes. He winked at her. Shocking how much earning her trust meant to him.

Wade laughed. "Looks like she approves."

"I almost forgot." Clint smacked his thigh. "I'll be right back." He jogged off in the direction of his truck.

Marshall ambled over to Ruby and crouched next to her. "I don't know if you like candy, but I brought you some just in case." He handed her a small white sack. She stared up at him through wide eyes and held the bag. He pointed to it. "Go ahead. You can open it."

She gulped but made no move to open the bag.

"Maybe later." He smiled at her and rose.

Clint loped back, slightly out of breath, and handed Ruby a stuffed brown horse. "From Lexi and me. Welcome home, Ruby."

She hugged the horse to her chest but didn't say anything.

Nash went over and lifted her into his arms. "What do you say, RuRu?"

"Thanks." The word was barely audible.

"Now I feel like a jerk. I didn't bring her anything." Wade sighed, kicking at the dirt. "Ruby, would you like a real pony? I can get you one. Just say the word."

"Wade! You can't promise her a pony!" Nash rolled his eyes skyward.

"I like ponies." Ruby's lashes curled up, revealing innocent and hopeful blue-green eyes.

Wade got close and kept his voice low. "I'll talk to your dad about it. Don't you worry. Next time I come, I'll bring you something real nice, sweetheart."

"You don't have to bring gifts," Nash said, although it warmed his heart they all cared.

"I want to. This pretty little thing should have a nice gift from her uncle Wade. I never thought I'd be an uncle."

"You could get married and have a few kids of your own." Clint grinned.

"No way. Not me. Married, kids—you fooling?" Wade let out a loud laugh. "All this talk is making me hungry. Who's up for pizza? I'm starving."

"I'm in," Marshall said.

"Same here." Clint pulled his keys out of his pocket, and they began making their way to their trucks.

"We'll be out in a minute. Let me grab Ruby's coat." Nash and Ruby walked hand in hand toward the house. Wade's comment about never getting married or having kids had been Nash's motto for a decade. Now that he had Ruby, he couldn't say *never*. God had given him a precious gift with this little girl. But marriage? He'd wanted one woman, and he couldn't have her.

One precious gift was enough in a lifetime. He'd make the most of what he had and not think about what he didn't. It was the only way he'd gotten this far in life. It was the only way he'd make it through the rest.

Chapter Five

"Howdy, puddin'!" With a pen tucked behind her ear, Dottie Lavert stopped in front of their booth at Dottie's Diner. Amy wasn't sure how she'd gotten the nickname puddin', but Dottie had been calling her that her entire life. "Hope you're keeping hotshot in line here, and, land's sake, if it isn't little buttercup."

Amy pressed her lips together to keep from laughing. She'd forgotten Dottie called Nash hotshot. Apparently, Ruby was buttercup. This would be the second time the three of them were out in public together. Would the people in town assume Amy had gotten back together with him?

Let them think what they wanted. She knew the truth. Besides, she doubted anyone even remembered she'd dated Nash all those years ago.

She was here for Ruby. Unfortunately, Amy hadn't made much progress with the child to this point. It wasn't as if she'd spent a ton of time with her, though. Ruby would get used to her. Eventually.

Nash, sitting across from her and Ruby, shimmied out of the booth and gave Dottie a big hug, lifting her off her feet. "Missed you, lil' mama."

"I just saw you a few days ago. It sure is good to have you back, hon." Her smile grew from ear to ear. Nash lowered her to the ground then took a seat. She dabbed under her misty eyes before getting down to business. "Okay, kids, what'll it be?"

Amy trailed her finger down the laminated menu until she found the kids' section. Turning to Ruby, she asked, "Do you like hamburgers? Or hot dogs? The chicken fingers are good."

"If you're in the mood for breakfast, I can make a stack of flapjacks with whipped cream on top, buttercup." Dottie's pen was poised above her small pad of paper. "And some crispy bacon. How does that sound?"

Ruby nodded.

"Are you sure?" Amy asked her. "If you'd rather have something else…"

"Whip cream," Ruby said decisively.

Amy caught Nash's eye. He shrugged, grinning.

Oh, my. His smile had always done her in. Her heart was beating way too fast. She pretended to study the menu.

Nash ordered a double cheeseburger with fries, and Amy took a chance on the daily special. The diner's home cooking was always delicious, but she wasn't all that hungry.

"Mom told me Dooley Hill has kittens needing homes." Amy looked at Nash. "Might be something to consider, you know, if your barn has mice."

"Uh-huh. Mice. Sure." He glanced around the diner.

Ruby tapped Amy's arm. "Do kitties live in barns? Do they eat mice?"

"Some do." She shifted to see Ruby better. "And some live in people's houses. They're called house cats. They curl up on your lap and purr and go potty in a litter box. But cats are independent. They aren't like puppies. You have to let them warm up to you."

"Oh."

"Why? Do you think you'd like a kitten of your own?"

"Yes." She wasn't jumping up and down in her seat or anything, but her eyes held hope—so much hope. Amy wanted to squish the child to her chest and never let her go. Ruby turned to Nash. "Daddy, could I have a kitten?"

He didn't answer. In fact, he seemed awfully distracted. Amy frowned. Either that or he didn't want to be seen with her. She waved to get Nash's attention. "Nash."

"Hmm?"

"There are tiger-striped kittens and a black-and-white one. They won't be weaned for another month, but if you're interested, I'll let Dooley know."

"A cat?" He grimaced. "What would we want one of those for, RuRu?"

"I like kitties." The simple words were innocent, straightforward.

"Litter boxes get stinky. Might need rubber gloves to deal with it. I don't know…"

"I'll clean it, Daddy."

"We'll have to think about it." Nash excused himself to say hi to someone who'd walked in.

Disappointment at his lack of interest coiled inside her. Was she boring him?

"I like any color kitty, Miss Amy," she said earnestly.

"I do, too." She pushed her irritation away and concentrated on Ruby. "If you had to choose, though, which would be your favorite?"

"The fluffiest." Her *l*'s sounded like *w*'s.

"I'll tell you what, I'll ask Dooley which is the fluff-iest. Then if your daddy says you can have a kitten, Dooley will save it for you. Now, why don't we draw while they cook our food?" Amy picked up the crayons Dottie had dropped off. She selected the red one and handed the small box to Ruby. Flipping over her paper placemat, she drew a tree and a sun.

Ruby watched. "Can you draw a horsey?"

"I can try." She sketched a rough outline of a horse, pleased the topic had loosened Ruby's tongue. Maybe Ruby was getting used to her. "What color would you like it?"

"Brown." Ruby handed her a crayon.

"I have an idea." Amy gave her the brown crayon back. "Why don't you color it in?"

"I'm no good." She put the crayon on the table, ducking her chin.

"Why do you say that?" Amy stretched her neck to try to see Ruby's face. "You don't have to be good at coloring. It's fun. You can scribble or stay in the lines. It's up to you."

"I'll get in trouble." Ruby glanced up. "Bad girls scribble."

"No. You won't get in trouble for coloring or scrib-bling. Not with me. Why don't you try?" Amy held her breath as Ruby's fingers inched toward the crayon. She picked it up, checking Amy's reaction. She nod-ded to her. "Go ahead. Color anywhere on the paper you'd like."

Ruby clutched the crayon in her fist. Amy made a mental note to show her the proper way to hold a pencil later. As Ruby brought the crayon to the placemat, Amy inwardly urged her on, but the tiny brown dot Ruby made must have spooked her. She dropped the crayon and backed into the corner of the booth.

"Where's Daddy?" Her voice held a tremor.

"He'll be right back." Had Ruby been punished for coloring? Amy scrambled to come up with her next move. She pointed to the brown line. "What a great start. I think I'll color a cloud on my paper."

Amy took the red crayon and drew a cloud. Then, with the green crayon, she filled it in, purposely scribbling outside the lines. "There. Perfect."

Ruby scooted closer. "Clouds aren't green."

"Today my cloud is green. Sometimes I draw yellow clouds or pink ones. That's the fun of coloring. You can make things whatever shade you'd like." Their drinks arrived, and she thanked Dottie before turning back to Ruby. "Did you get in trouble for coloring?"

She hung her head.

"When you're learning to do something, you don't have to be perfect. It doesn't always come out the way you want. But you keep trying and you get better. It's okay to make mistakes. Like scissors—have you ever cut anything?"

"I cut the tater bag open."

Amy had to refrain from putting her arm around her. A potato bag. She could only imagine why a small child would need to open a bag of potatoes. She had the urge to tell Dottie to double the whipped cream on those flapjacks and bring an extra serving on the side, as well.

"Tuesday I'll bring some safety scissors, and I'll teach you how to cut paper. We can make a paper chain."

Amy continued to color as she watched Ruby from the corner of her eye. The child was discreetly tucking sugar packets into her pockets. Should she say something? All that raw sugar wasn't good for anyone. Nash's warning about hoarding food hadn't included any advice. Should she tell Ruby to put the packets back?

Nash returned, sliding into the booth. "Sorry about that. I've been trying to reach a local farrier, and Clint told me I could probably catch him here today. What did I miss?"

"Nothing much. Just coloring." Amy's annoyance returned. Surely Nash could have called and left a message with the farrier. He knew how difficult it had been for Ruby to be alone with Amy before.

Now she was just being petty. She wanted to confide in him about the sugar packets and coloring situation, but it wasn't the time.

"Did I tell you I've got the horses out to pasture? Wade, Clint and Marshall came out yesterday to help."

"I got a pony!" Ruby's eyes lit up like fireworks.

"A pony?" Amy plastered a grin on her face although she wasn't sure itty-bitty Ruby was ready for a pony. "What color is it?"

"Brown and it has a white dot on its head."

"It's not a real pony. Not yet, at least." Nash winked at Ruby. "Did you decide on a name?"

"Brownie."

"Brownie?" Nash pulled a face. Amy almost warned him not to say anything, that Ruby could name her horse anything she wanted. "Now you've got me hungry for brownies with chocolate frosting and sprinkles all over them."

Amy relaxed. Her fear had been for nothing. Nash always seemed to know exactly what to say to Ruby. Maybe she was being too hard on him for his apparent lack of interest today.

"Good name," Amy said. "I can't wait to meet this Brownie."

Dottie set huge plates of food in front of them. "Y'all just holler if you need anything. Is that enough whipped cream, buttercup?"

With shining eyes, Ruby nodded to her.

"You tell your daddy to bring you around more often." Dottie turned to Nash. "Seeing as you've got time on your hands, you should stop by Monday morning. Big Bob, Jerry Cornell from Rock Step Ranch and Stan Reynolds have a standing coffee date every Monday at seven thirty. They'd love to catch up with you. Buttercup can have breakfast at the counter with me while you gab."

Amy spread a paper napkin across her lap, certain Nash would never in a million years agree to have coffee with three old-timers. He'd always resented authority.

"Thanks, lil' mama. I'll be here."

Amy almost choked. Nash hanging out with Big Bob, Jerry and Stan? Did she know him at all anymore? Obviously not.

"Want me to cut your pancakes for you, Ruby?" Amy reached over to slice them into small squares. The melting whipped cream slid to the side. "By the way, the church is having an Easter egg hunt next Saturday. Maybe we could all go together."

Nash squirted ketchup on his plate. "Ooh, that's a great idea. RuRu, I'll help you find the eggs if you'll give me all your Snickers bars."

"What's Snickers?" Ruby nibbled on her bacon.

"Just the most delicious candy bar on the planet." He grabbed the burger with both hands and met Amy's eyes. "You still coming this Tuesday?"

"Yes. Ruby and I have plans to make paper chains. I'll come over Thursday, too."

His face brightened in relief. Maybe he was just having a hard time adjusting to fatherhood. His move back could be difficult for him, too. Which made her wonder…how much of Nash's humor was an act for Ruby's sake? And what was it costing him? She'd known him once, but this man had a lot of layers she didn't recognize.

He could keep his layers. She didn't need to know him. He certainly didn't seem all that interested in getting to know her.

His brain might get addled if he didn't get out and socialize more often. Nash watched the countryside pass by on his way to town Monday morning. In her car seat behind him, Ruby clutched Brownie. Church yesterday had been a relief. He'd reconnected with a few people he recognized from high school, and he'd enjoyed introducing Ruby. Sure, a small crowd formed around him afterward, and he'd signed a few autographs, but he was used to it. Had been signing autographs for years.

The only downside to church had been his distraction during the service itself. Amy had sat with her parents on the other side, three pews up. He'd tried not to stare at all the dark hair cascading down her back, but time and again he'd failed. Maybe if he had something to do with his days besides taking care of Ruby, he'd have less time to linger on his memories of Amy.

For years he'd been busy traveling, competing and keeping up with the business side of his career. Stripped of the hustle-bustle, his life now loomed wide open, and the solitude was getting to him. He missed having a purpose. Missed the camaraderie with his bull riding buddies.

That's why he'd latched on to Dottie's invitation to join her husband and the other guys. He'd always admired Big Bob Lavert. Shortly after Hank had died, Nash had been sent to Yearling Group Home for teen boys. Big Bob and Dottie had run Yearling, and they'd been more parents to him than his own warped mother, who'd been incarcerated at the time. Big Bob had taught him how a man of integrity acted.

Sometimes Nash still missed Hank. He'd never forget the summers he'd spent with his mother's ex-boyfriend. He'd learned everything he'd needed to know about competing in rodeos from the cowboy, and the training had launched his career. Although Hank had been a compulsive gambler and an alcoholic, he'd gotten Nash out of the terror of living with his mother for three months every year. For that, Nash would be eternally grateful.

He turned onto Main Street and parked near Dottie's Diner. He got out and opened the back door to help Ruby. The wind was blowing strong this morning. As he lifted her up, she let out a cry, pointing to Brownie. He grabbed the horse and hurried them both inside.

"Whew. The weather is ornery today." He set Ruby down near the counter. She hopped onto a round, red vinyl–topped stool bolted to the floor. Dottie came out from the kitchen and grinned. Her light gray hair had poufy bangs and was twisted up in the back with a clip. He tipped his hat to her. "Hey, lil' mama."

"The fellas are back there. I'll take a break with buttercup here." She leaned over the counter in front of Ruby. "I made some waffles. You like them?"

Ruby, beaming, nodded.

"Good. I think a glass of chocolate milk will help them go down. What do you think?"

Nash squeezed Ruby's shoulder. "I'll be right over there if you need me. Remember what we talked about—don't take the sugar packets. Oh, and make sure that horse stays in line."

"What have I always said about horses in my diner? None allowed." Dottie crossed her arms over her ample chest. "Oh, wait. Are you talking about the one you're holding? He looks harmless enough. He can stay."

Ruby hugged Brownie tightly.

"I'm just teasing ya, buttercup. I'll be right back with the food."

Nash headed to the booth in the back where the men were drinking coffee and laughing about something. Big Bob started to get up, but Nash waved him down.

"Dottie said you might join us, but we didn't know if you'd show up." Big Bob looked bigger and older than Nash remembered, but his eyes were shrewd and kind. "Fellas, this is Nash Bolton, two-time PBR world champion, Touring Pro Division champion and runner up at the World Finals. He also rode the meanest bull alive and lived to tell about it. Nash, I don't know if you remember Jerry Cornell and Stan Reynolds."

"Good to see you again." Nash shook their hands and slid into the booth next to Stan.

"What was riding Murgatroyd really like?" Jerry leaned forward. His wiry frame reminded Nash of Hank and the cowboys he'd spent all those years with. He'd toured with the best of them.

"It was like trying to hop on a comet," Nash said. "That rotten bull lit me up good."

"Oh-ho! You hear that, Stan? A comet." Looking pleased with himself, Jerry sat back and slurped his coffee.

"I heard you, Jerry. Don't get all smug. I never said Murgatroyd was easy."

"You implied it. Didn't he compare the beast to a dairy cow, Big Bob?"

"You did, Stan, and it's time you eat those words."

"I'm not eating nothing." Stan threw his wadded up napkin on the table. "I don't care what you say. Night Fright is meaner and bigger than Murgatroyd."

Nash sat back in his seat, thoroughly enjoying this exchange. This had been what he'd missed for months—smack talk mixed with an obsession of all things rodeo.

"Well, Nash rode Night Fright, too, so let's get his opinion," Big Bob said. All three men looked at Nash expectantly.

"Night Fright is a tremendous bull. Strong. Cunning. He knows all the riders' tricks. But I figured him out. Rode him the full eight seconds and then some. Murgatroyd, on the other hand..."

An awed silence descended for a moment.

"You see?" Jerry smacked his hand on the table. "Night Fright isn't all he's cracked up to be, so you can stop yammerin' on about him."

Stan glared. "He just said he's strong and cunning."

"You know what bull to really watch out for?" Nash made sure he'd caught their attention. When they'd leaned in, he continued. "Trombone."

"Trombone," they echoed.

"He'll be the one to beat in another year or two."

"You don't say?" Stan pulled a small box out of his chest pocket and tapped out a toothpick.

Big Bob gestured for the waitress to bring Nash a cup of coffee. "You hungry, son?"

The waitress poured a cup, and Nash ordered eggs, home fries and sausage patties.

"How you liking that property?" Jerry asked. "You're out near Four Forks Road, right?"

"Love it." Nash took a sip of the piping hot brew. "I think Ruby's going to be a little country girl. She's happy out there."

"I hear you got your horses in," Big Bob said. "You gonna put up more fence?"

"I'm going to have to. I need more pasture. Who do I talk to about installing some?"

"Roscoe Lovey," Jerry said. "He's the best around. Fastest, too. You putting up cattle?"

"No. I'm not sure what I'm doing yet. Been thinking about maybe… Nah, never mind." He felt the heat rising up his neck. Why was it so hard to admit he'd been thinking about teaching kids how to ride bulls?

"What were you going to say?" Stan sucked on the end of the toothpick.

"I'd have to wait until Ruby's in school, anyway, but…I've been thinking about opening a training center. Teaching kids how to ride bulls."

The three men stared at each other for a second then turned as one to him. Their grinning faces told him what he hadn't dared expect. The idea was good.

"That's the best plan I've heard in a long time," Jerry said. "Some of these kids are like pronghorns running across the plains. Smart but skittish. If they had someone teaching 'em proper, they'd have a shot at the big time."

"I agree with Jerry," Big Bob said. "Having someone like you show them the ropes would make a big difference."

"I'm not sure," Nash said, toying with his coffee mug.

"You should at least talk to Billy Jacobs. He took over the high school rodeo program last year. I'm sure he could use some help if you wouldn't mind sparing a bit of your free time. Might give you an idea if working with kids is for you."

"I'll consider it. I've definitely got plenty of free time." Talking to the high school coach might be smart. Something still held him back, though. "I don't know if I should encourage anyone to ride bulls. Doctors wanted me to retire about seventy-two times. It's dangerous. I'm beat-up, and I'm only thirty-one."

"They're going to ride anyway, Nash." Big Bob leaned back, his hands on his impressive stomach. "You could help them avoid the injuries."

Nash frowned. "There's no avoiding the injuries. It's the most dangerous sport in the world for a reason."

"That's why it's so excitin'." Jerry got a faraway look in his eyes. "Makes me feel alive watching you young bucks get in the chute. Wish I was younger, so I could take a ride myself."

"Well, I'm thinking about it, but I'm not committing to it. Not yet, anyway."

"If you need help, we'll be over." Stan flicked the toothpick onto his plate.

"That's right," Big Bob said. "You need anything, just holler."

"Thanks," Nash said. "I might take you up on it. I'll keep you posted."

The other men started discussing the bull riding sea-son, and he looked over his shoulder at Ruby. Dottie was pretending Brownie was trotting on the counter. His chest swelled. He hadn't had a home in ten years. Hadn't really had one before that either, with all the traveling he'd done even as a teen. But with this community, he could give one to Ruby. The Lord had blessed them.

Amy's pretty face came to mind.

What if he messed this—living in Sweet Dreams near her—up?

He couldn't. Not this time.

Saturday morning Amy searched the crowded church lawn for Nash and Ruby. Everywhere she looked stood happy families. Young mothers holding babies. Dads playing with toddlers. Grandparents smiling as school-age kids chased each other. Everyone seemed to be tending to small children. Everyone except her. The ache in her chest grew, and it had already been gnawing at her since opening her mailbox earlier.

She'd ripped open the envelope from a fabric manufacturer and read the dreaded words, "We regret to inform you…doesn't meet our needs at this time."

Rejected.

All these awful feelings of incompetency had flooded her, and they hadn't left. It was as if a bully was chanting, *What did you expect? You didn't actually think you were good enough to have your own fabric line, did you?*

She could actually feel her face falling. She pasted her smile back on. No one needed to know she'd failed. God knew best. Maybe she wasn't meant to have a fabric line.

A man bumped into her, his towheaded toddler giggling from his perch on the man's shoulders. The guy apologized. She murmured she was fine.

But she wasn't fine.

No fabric line. No family of her own.

Oh, God, help me not want these things so much.

She spotted Nash in his cowboy hat, and her spirits sank lower. His eyes crinkled with laughter, and he was signing a paper someone held out for him. Autographing things for his fans.

Ugh. He had it all. The adoring crowd, the career he'd always wanted and a beautiful girl to raise as his own.

It wasn't fair.

Nash caught her eye and hitched his chin for her to come over. She almost rolled her eyes. A dozen people crowded around him. What did he need her for? She certainly wasn't going to ask him for an autograph. She debated going back to her car and driving to Lexi's for a whine session.

But then she spotted Ruby, and the child had that blank look on her face Amy had come to know all too well. This crowd probably scared the sweetheart. Amy hurried over to where they stood.

"Hey, Ruby, why don't you come over here? We need to get your plastic bag." Amy held her hand out, not knowing if Ruby would take it. Although Amy had spent Tuesday and Thursday with her making paper chains and reading picture books, Ruby still shied away from physical contact. To her surprise, Ruby gripped her hand and huddled next to her legs. Amy crouched down to look her in the eyes. "What's wrong, honey? Are you okay?"

Ruby's bottom lip pushed forward, and she gave her head a small shake.

"Come on. We'll get your bag and sit over there until the egg hunt starts. No one will bother us." Amy led her by the hand to the table set up near the sidewalk.

"Well, hello, Amy. My subway tile quilt is going much better than the dresden plate design. I don't know what I was thinking, taking on such a complicated pattern. Thanks for helping me. I see you've brought a friend to the egg hunt." Mrs. Jenkins, a retired librarian with short white hair and a welcoming face, handed Ruby a plastic grocery bag. "What's your name, sweetie?"

Ruby's hand tightened in Amy's.

"This is Ruby Bolton, Mrs. Jenkins." Amy gave the dear woman a big smile. "And this is her first Easter egg hunt, so I'm going to give her some pointers."

"Oh, right, Nash's little girl." Mrs. Jenkins gestured toward the church landscaping. "Look over there. Hope you get lots of eggs, Ruby. Don't let those boys push you around. Check under the bushes, too."

"Thanks, we'll keep that in mind." Amy led Ruby to a patch of grass on the outskirts of the lawn. Then she sat down cross-legged and, to her shock, Ruby sat in her lap. Amy closed her eyes, savoring the moment. *Thank You, God.*

"I never hunted eggs." Ruby stretched her neck back to see Amy. "Are they real?"

"No, honey. They're plastic. Each one has a surprise inside. That's why it's so fun."

"What if someone steals 'em all? Will the boys take mine?" She seemed on the verge of tears.

"There are lots of eggs here. I'll hold your hand the entire time, okay? I won't let anything happen to you or your eggs."

Ruby leaned back to rest against Amy's chest. Amy had to remind herself to breathe. This precious little girl finally trusted her enough to sit in her lap. Amy wrapped both arms around her, giving her a small hug. It didn't matter Ruby wasn't her child. This was almost as good. Before long a whistle blew.

"It's going to begin soon. We'd better go to the start- ing line." They walked hand in hand to the orange line someone had spray-painted on the lawn. Using a bull- horn, the pastor told everyone the rules. Nash loped over to them.

"Sorry about that." His eyes were all apologies to Amy.

She drew her shoulders back. She wasn't sure how she felt about him being a celebrity in Sweet Dreams. Did he care more about his fans than keeping an eye on Ruby? He should have noticed how upset she was. Maybe Mom was right and the lure of the limelight was why he'd left.

He rubbed his hands together and said to Ruby, "Are you ready to find some eggs?"

"Miss Amy's helping me. Don't let boys steal my eggs, Daddy."

He gave Amy a questioning look, but she didn't elab- orate.

"I'll string up anyone who dares think about taking your eggs." He cracked his knuckles. Children and their parents crammed next to them behind the line, every- one waiting for the hunt to begin.

"On your mark. Get set. Go!"

All the kids ran, scattering in different directions. "This way, Ruby." Amy guided her to the shrubs around the church. Ruby saw a pink egg and quickly scooped it up. She held it in her hand as if it were pure gold.

"Oh, I see another one." Nash pointed to the birdbath. Ruby ran over and grabbed the purple egg.

Amy held the bag open, and Ruby dropped it in. She saw another one, but a little boy found it before she got there, and her eyes filled with tears.

"Not all of the eggs are for you, RuRu. They're for all the kids."

"Let's check over here, Ruby. Not many kids went this way." Amy held her hand as a few tears dropped, but when Ruby saw three eggs in the grass, she tore away and practically dove on them. Then she cradled them to her chest, her face triumphant.

"I got them!" She dumped them into the bag, too. They searched for several more minutes, finding eggs here and there before calling it quits. The three of them returned to the lawn near the parking lot and sat on the grass with the other families.

As Nash showed Ruby how to open the eggs, Amy memorized the look of wonder on her face when candy or stickers or erasers fell out. Ruby shoved as many pieces of candy in her pockets as they would hold and left everything else in the plastic bag, which she gripped tightly. Soon everyone headed to the small pavilion for hot dogs and chips.

With full plates, Amy and Nash sat across from each other at the picnic table. Ruby, next to Nash, couldn't stop peeking inside her bag full of prizes. Moments later Amy noticed the girl slip her hot dog into the bag.

"Ruby, why don't you eat your hot dog now?" She kept her tone light. "It won't be good if you try to save it for later."

Ruby's eyes filled with tears.

"Oh, don't cry, honey." Amy's spirits slid to the ground. "I didn't mean to hurt your feelings. I don't want you getting sick. That's all."

"Miss Amy's right. Food spoils, RuRu. You don't want a tummyache."

With a few sad sniffs, Ruby pulled the hot dog out of the bag. Nash teased Ruby, telling her she needed a pile of onions on her dog.

You made Ruby cry. You didn't sell your fabrics. You might never be a mother. You don't have a husband and kids like the other women here. Something is wrong with you.

Why were these thoughts attacking her now? She'd made peace with being single. She could live a happy life without children. She was thankful for the time with Ruby.

"Is something wrong, Amy?" Nash asked quietly.

Her neck grew warm. She couldn't admit she was feeling sorry for herself. Without thinking it through, she blurted out, "I heard from a fabric manufacturer earlier. They passed on my designs."

He stopped chewing midchip. "I'm sorry to hear that."

Not trusting herself to speak, she nodded. He really did seem sorry.

"Send the designs to a different company. You've got a lot of talent. Someone will want them."

"Four other companies have my portfolio. It was just…"

"A blow. I know." From his tone, she believed him.

Her emotions were entering dangerous territory. She gathered her empty plate and napkin.

"Hang in there. You'll sell the fabrics. God has a plan for you."

Stunned, she blinked. Had Nash Bolton just given her spiritual advice? He'd never been one for prayer or talking about the Lord when they'd dated.

He'd grown up.

And she didn't really know the man across from her. Aside from when she'd arrived, he'd given her and Ruby his full attention, even when people approached him in the food line.

"Amy?" Nash asked. She shook her thoughts away. "Find out if your friend still has one of those kittens. We've decided to brave the kitty litter."

Why emotion welled up, she had no idea, but she forced herself to smile. "I'll tell him to save the fluffiest one for you."

Their eyes met and understanding wove between them. She stood, looking for a trash can.

She'd never been one to share her feelings with the world, not even her closest friends. She figured they didn't need to be burdened with her petty problems. But Nash had always been able to read her.

He still cared enough to ask.

And if he cared enough to ask…

He might not be the monster she preferred him to be. Or maybe that's how he did it—got foolish girls like her to care about him. All thoughtful and charming until it didn't suit him and something better came along.

Tossing her empty plate in the trash with more force than necessary, she scolded herself.

She wasn't a girl, and she wasn't a fool, and she wasn't falling for him this time. She'd grown up, too.

Chapter Six

"**D**on't let her go too far." The mid-May breeze rippled through Amy's hair as she watched Ruby play with the kitten in Nash's backyard. A lazy Saturday afternoon—perfect for introducing the cat to her new home.

Funny how time changed things. It had been over a month since the Easter egg hunt. The weather had warmed, and Amy had grown less guarded around Nash. They'd settled into a sort of truce, where neither brought up the past and they both kept an emotional distance. As much as she wanted it to stay that way, this surface friendship kept poking holes in the emotional baggage she'd thought she'd unpacked. Questions about why he'd left kept bubbling up. She didn't know how much longer she could press them down.

Nash was in the house getting iced tea for them. The kitten had already inspected every nook and cranny of her new home and gotten into a bit of trouble when she'd squeezed her tiger-striped body behind the dryer in the mudroom. That's why they'd brought the bundle of energy outside for a while.

"Have you decided on a name yet?" Amy leaned

back against her hands as she sat on the grass with her legs out in front of her.

"Not yet, Miss Amy." Ruby's delight switched to worry.

"Why don't you pick a few names to choose from?" Amy had learned how Ruby's mind worked. The child was terrified of making mistakes, and she struggled to make decisions. The imaginative play most children engaged in was something to be feared in Ruby's world, but Amy was doing her best to make her feel safe. And, thankfully, she was slowly becoming more playful and less insecure. She'd even gotten better about not tucking away food for later.

"Okay." Ruby appeared to be deep in thought. The kitten pounced on a weed in the grass. "We could name her Tiger."

"You could." Amy bit her tongue, wishing Ruby would take a chance on a less safe name. "What other ones do you have?"

The kitten darted off after a butterfly. Ruby shrieked, chasing her. She picked her up under her front arms then scooped up her bottom the way Amy had shown her, clutching the cat to her chest. "Bad kitty. Don't run off."

"Maybe we should bring the kitten back inside for a while." Amy stood, brushing off her jeans, and waited for Ruby to join her. From the patio, they went through the dining area to the living room. Yawning, Ruby sat on the couch and kept the wiggly cat on her lap.

"I was just coming out to join you." Nash handed Amy a glass of iced tea. "Did you name the creature yet, RuRu?"

"Fluffy." With Ruby's lisp, it sounded like Fwuffy.

Amy had to choke down a laugh. The girl was too adorable. And Fluffy was slightly more original than Tiger.

"Fluffy?" He scratched his chin. "How about Fleabag?"

"No, Daddy, it's Fluffy." She hopped off the couch,
cat in her arms, and headed toward the staircase. "I'm
playing with her in my room."

Amy tucked her lips under in amusement at Nash's
raised eyebrows. *Good for you, Ruby.* She'd stood her
ground.

"Well, that's a first," he said. "She's never played in
her room by herself before."

"She's not by herself. She's with Fluffy."

"If I'd known getting her a cat would solve that problem, I would have gotten one earlier. Thanks for bringing it over." He gestured to the patio. "Want to drink
these outside? It's too nice out to be stuck in here."

"Sure." She carried her drink to the wrought iron
table and sank into the cushions of one of the matching chairs.

One nice thing about spending time with Nash and
Ruby? Amy no longer had the prickly sensation, the
one shouting for her to be on high alert, when she was
near him. Growing comfortable around him was probably inevitable with all the crafts and activities she and
Ruby did every week in his kitchen. The three of them
had ventured to other places, too, including story time
at the library and a visit to Lexi and Clint's ranch.

"I see the fence is coming along." She pointed to the
trucks in the distance. A work crew had been there all
week, installing posts.

"Yep. I want the horses to have lots of room to roam."
He got a faraway look in his eye. "Hank used to tell me

in a perfect world retired horses would have plenty of pasture and the freedom to run. Then he'd toss his cigarette butt on the ground, twist it under his cowboy boot and say too bad it wasn't a perfect world."

"Who's Hank?" Amy sipped her tea. Probably a guy he'd worked with when riding bulls.

His grave expression made her pause.

"Hank was the closest thing to a father I had growing up. He was the one who got me into riding bulls as a kid."

She didn't mean to stare at him, but Nash's childhood details had been off limits to her in the past. Habit almost made her suppress her questions. But she wasn't his girlfriend. Had nothing to lose by asking them now. And she wanted some answers.

"How old were you?" she asked.

"Must have been a couple years older than Ruby." He didn't look at her, but his easy tone didn't fool her. He was nervous.

"How did you know him?"

He let out a loud sigh. "Do you really want to hear all this? It was a long time ago."

"Yeah, why not?" She tried to sound nonchalant, but tension lined her words. She wanted to know more. When they'd dated she'd trusted he would tell her things in his own time, and she'd been content not to press. But he'd never told her...and now that he was back and they were getting along okay...she wanted to fill in some of the gaps. To understand him better so she wouldn't put him on a pedestal the way she had originally.

"Hank and my mother dated for a while. That summer we lived in a beat-up camper. Traveled to every rinky-dink rodeo in Wyoming for Hank to ride bulls and earn a little dough. I was his helper. I'd muck stalls and take care of the horses while he and my mother paid the entry fees and found their party for the night. I got to hang out with the other rodeo kids, and before I knew it I was riding calves, too."

"Wait a minute." Amy was doing the math in her head. "You were only about six, right? You were taking care of the horses while they found a party? What exactly does that mean?"

He shrugged, kicking his feet up onto the empty chair next to him, one cowboy boot crossed over the other. "Hank and my mother liked to drink, and Hank was a gambler."

"Where were you when all this was going on?" She tapped the table with her fingertips. Maybe she was reading too much into it, but it sounded a bit much for a child barely in elementary school.

"Oh, I was having the time of my life. I had three meals a day. Got to brush and feed the horses. And once Hank saw me winning belts, he told me everything he knew about riding bulls."

She pursed her lips. The time of his life? Running wild, more like it.

"He and my mother broke up—no surprise there— when summer ended. The Friday night rodeos closed, so Hank drove us back to our old apartment and left. It was a bad time for me."

"You never saw him again?" Although the man sounded like a bad influence, she sympathized with Nash just the same. He clearly cared for the guy.

"I thought he was out of our lives for good. That's the way it was with most of my mother's men, but the following May, Hank showed up at the dump we were living in and made a deal with my mother. He wanted me to join him for the summer. She'd get half of any earnings I made from competing, and Hank would keep the other half. She agreed. I think she was glad to have me off her hands."

"So you were their money maker? You were a small child."

He laughed, his cowboy hat tipping over his eyes. He pushed it back. "Not yet. No, it would be another year before I was winning enough to make it worth his while."

"Then why did he do it? Take you with him?"

Nash shrugged, a faraway look in his eyes. "He wasn't good alone. I took care of the horses, woke him up in time to get sober and ride and made sure we both ate. He was a chain smoker, an alcoholic, a gambler. He was tough on me. He'd lick me good if I came in second. Then he'd explain exactly what I'd done wrong. That's why I cared about him. Idolized him. No one ever gave a nickel about me except Hank. I spent every summer with him until I was thirteen years old, and I was making a lot of money for him by then. When I wasn't competing on the bulls, I rode his horses in other events."

"You were making money for him? Didn't you get to keep any?" This Hank guy sounded awful, but she could kind of understand why a kid like Nash would like him.

"He sent some back to my mother—never the half he'd promised her—and he'd tell me he was on a winning streak and that he'd double the money and give me a cut. He gambled everything away. Every night. It was an addiction."

She thought of her own father and how he'd raised her and her brother. He was the one who'd provided for them, not the other way around. Fondness colored Nash's words, and she could see in his tender expression he didn't hold anything against Hank.

"You loved him, didn't you?"

He turned to her. "Yeah, I did. I wanted him to be my father. I even asked him if he was, but he'd been in jail for two years when I was born, so it wasn't physically possible."

Nash's words weeks ago about not knowing his father came to mind. She hadn't considered how that must have affected him. To not know who his father was… her heart twisted. He'd had a difficult childhood, and she hadn't really known it. Maybe she hadn't pushed for more information years ago because deep down she hadn't wanted to know.

"What happened when you turned thirteen?" She sipped her iced tea.

"Hank died."

She choked, coughing. "How?"

"He was blowing through so much money. I could feel his anxieties intensifying. He wasn't much of a barrel racer, but he'd signed up for extra events to bring in cash. The night he died no one knew he'd been drinking to get his courage up for the performance. He hid it well, but his reflexes were slow. He turned the first barrel and the horse bucked him off before landing on him. Broke Hank's neck. Killed him instantly."

"Oh, no." Amy reached across the table, covering his hand with hers. "I'm so sorry."

Nash's jaw shifted. He seemed to be getting his emotions under control. "Yeah, well, what do you do? I went back to my mother, but she wasn't there."

Amy could barely keep up. First Hank died, and then his mother was gone? "Where was she?"

"In prison. She'd gotten caught selling drugs to minors near the high school in Sheridan, the town where we were living. Of course, she was also charged with possession. Since she already had a long police record, the judge didn't go easy on her to give the usual minimum sentence. She got seven years."

Amy shivered. Nash's childhood sounded like a horrible nightmare. When she was thirteen, she was going to sleepovers and doodling her crush's name in her journal. And Nash had to take care of some drunken gambler while his mom went to jail? Didn't seem fair.

"What happened to you then?"

"Hank was gone. My mother was gone. If I'd had my way, I would have been gone, too. I figured I'd do what I'd been doing—competing in rodeos in the summer to make enough money to take care of myself the rest of the year. I wanted to hire in as a ranch hand somewhere, but the government had other plans. I was sent here, to Yearling Group Home, instead."

A lump formed in her throat. He hadn't even been in high school yet, and he'd been prepared to work full-time to take care of himself? She studied his profile. Strong features, confident tilt to his head. She'd never guessed he'd gotten all his strength and confidence from such a messed up childhood. Compassion for him rose unbidden. How she wanted to shove it away, but she couldn't deny the pressure building inside her, the heavy sadness for the boy he'd been.

He turned to face her then, and his bleak eyes twisted her heart. She didn't want to care about him. If she did, she'd...

Don't feel sorry for him. Don't do it, Amy. If you want to feel sorry for someone, feel sorry for yourself from ten years ago. Remember the girl who could barely get out of bed after he left? Feel sorry for her.

"Yearling turned out great. I met Clint, Wade and Marshall there. And Big Bob cared about my rodeo aspirations. He hooked me up with his friend who competed on the summer rodeo circuit. My summers were tamer than they'd been with Hank, but I learned about discipline and doing the right thing. In many ways Big Bob made it possible for me to have my career." He took off his hat, raked his fingers through his hair and shoved it back on his head. "Enough about me. Tell me something good. How did you end up owning your own quilt store?"

Her life seemed so conventional and easy compared to his. It'd be simple to answer his question. Give him the safe tour of her life after he'd left. How she'd worked at a daycare during the day and started quilting at night. She could hide the fact she'd tried to lose her memories of him by stitching fabrics together. How every quilt she'd made had been a way to escape the devastation of him leaving her.

Or she could tell him the truth. Let him see that her life might have been tame, but her pain had cut deep.

She faced him. *Tell him the truth. Don't sugarcoat it to protect him.* He'd been honest with her. It was time she was honest with him.

"After you left, I—" her throat was so tight, she almost couldn't continue "—had a hard time with life. At first I thought you'd been in an accident or were in trouble or something. I couldn't imagine you would just…leave. No note. No call. No 'It's over.' No goodbye. I was scared for you. A week later when I saw in the paper you'd won an event, I had to accept reality. You'd left on purpose."

"Amy, I—"

She thrust her hand out. "No, nope. It isn't your turn. This is about me."

He grudgingly nodded.

"You were my best friend." Her eyes welled with tears. "I loved you. Cherished you. Thought nothing but the best of you. And then you were gone. I'd get home from the daycare and pick up the phone to tell you about something funny one of the kids said, and the receiver would drop out of my hand. You cut me out of your life, and mine became very empty."

He shifted in his seat, his face grave.

She shook away the threatening tears, swallowed the lump in her throat. "I didn't know what to do with myself. I couldn't sleep. Couldn't eat. Could barely breathe for weeks. Had no one to talk to—Lexi was off at college and we hadn't kept up with each other. Then one night, when I was about as low as a person can go, I started sewing scraps together. The rhythmic motion of the needle took my mind somewhere else."

He stood, pacing, his movements agitated and robotic. "I hate myself for that."

"I hated you, too." She rose also, rubbing her arms, and gazed at the barn in the distance. Maybe she shouldn't have told him. "I'm not trying to punish you. I just…well, I needed you to know."

He came up next to her. She dared not move or she'd fall apart. His shoulder was less than an inch from hers. All she'd have to do is lean ever so slightly and he'd put his arm around her like old times. And she remembered every detail of his arms around her—how safe she'd felt, how protected, how loved.

She squeezed her eyes shut. *Don't remember. Forget it. Forget it all.*

His arm crept over her shoulders. She hissed as she inhaled, craving his embrace and hating herself for still wanting it. She spun away from him.

"It's your fault, you know. The life I wanted? Gone. You shattered my dreams, Nash Bolton. You shattered them!"

He'd broken his cardinal rule.

He'd touched her. Soft, feminine familiar Amy. And now she was yelling at him.

Good.

He deserved her wrath. He'd been waiting for his punishment since the day he returned. And hearing her say he'd been her best friend broke something inside him. She'd been his, too. Not talking to her had been the hardest thing he'd ever done. Sometimes he'd picked up the phone, dialed half her number and hung up, his throat gripped with emotion. He'd wanted so badly to tell her about each event after it was over, the way he'd done when they were together.

He'd lost his best friend, the only person who'd ever thought the absolute best of him.

And he'd walk away again, given the same circumstances.

"I know it's my fault." He stepped back, widened his stance and hooked his thumbs in his belt loops. "I loved you."

"How can you say that? What you did was not love."

"Yes, it was. I—"

"I already told you—I don't want to hear it. There is no excuse why you couldn't have had the decency to break up with me first." She blinked back tears. "When you left, you took away my dream of a family."

He clenched his jaw. She wouldn't let him explain. Didn't want to hear his reasons. How could he get through to her if he couldn't explain?

"If you'd give me a chance, you might not think it was so lame." He stepped closer to her. The look in her eyes could have killed a rattler on the spot. His temper flared, too. "Fine. I won't tell you why I left. It's your right to refuse me. But don't blame me for not having a family. It's been over ten years. This might be a small town, but last time I checked there were plenty of single guys here. You could have married one of them and had a house full of babies. You can't blame everything on me, Amy."

"Well, I almost did marry one."

His heart ripped open. She'd fallen in love with someone else? He wanted to punch something, but he kept calm and quietly asked, "Who?"

"John McCloud."

"Don't know him." He had to refrain from cracking his knuckles. He wanted to find out everything about this guy, but what would be the point? It wasn't as if Nash had any say in the matter.

"You wouldn't know him." She stood her ground. "He was a bank manager. He moved here from Greybull several years ago. We dated for over a year. We talked about getting married and buying a little house in town."

He had no right to be jealous, but the thought of some guy making plans to marry Amy and live in a house right here in Sweet Dreams twisted his gut. It had been Nash's fondest wish for himself. He blinked away the emotions. Amy must have come to her senses and dropped the guy.

She averted her gaze. "He changed his mind. Moved down to Florida instead."

He frowned, trying to figure out what she meant.

"At least he had the decency to tell me before he left." She studied her fingernails. Her posture said, "I'm strong," but her face said otherwise.

Without thinking it through, Nash closed the short distance between them and wrapped his arms around her. The instant he registered her warm body next to his, he sighed. *This is what I've been missing. If I never have her in my arms again, I'll remember this and it will have to be enough.*

Her silky hair teased his cheek, and her fresh cookie smell weakened his resolve.

He wanted to kiss her.

He wouldn't. Couldn't.

But he wanted to.

She stepped away from him. "You're right. I can't blame you for how my life turned out." She slowly pivoted, looking out at the yard. "And I'm happy with my life, Nash. I have a successful business. Good friends. I'm very happy."

He wasn't dense. He knew what she was saying. She was happy—very happy—without him in her life.

He wished he could say the same.

How his body craved riding a bucking bull for eight seconds and hitting the dirt floor of the arena. Going through the mental checklist of possible injuries as he scrambled out of harm's way had been like scratching an itch.

Right now he had a powerful itch.

He frowned. Why would those minutes when he'd scampered to safety, assessing any pain in his body, give him relief in any way?

"Were you happy, Nash?" Amy asked quietly.

He didn't know how to answer that. All the reasons he'd thought he'd gone into bull riding might not be true. Sure, he'd wanted to be the best. Yeah, he wanted to be someone other than the son of a prostitute and drug addict. He'd had dreams of big money and fame. And he'd gotten it all.

But what if he'd competed all those years for something else? What if happiness had never been on the list?

"Sure," he said gruffly. "I loved the excitement, the danger, the thrill of the ride."

All true. Except deep down, he feared he finally understood why he'd been compelled to ride the meanest bulls, to stay on the longest.

Had he been punishing himself? For being a nothing kid, for having a mess of a mom, for losing Hank?

Whether she knew it or not, Amy had always been better off without him.

Why, oh why, had Nash gone and held her? She'd been doing so well. Keeping her focus on Ruby. Ignoring the past. Making pleasantries with Nash. Not getting too close. And then she'd blown it. Worse, she couldn't get her mind off it. Even church yesterday hadn't been enough to clear her head.

"I messed up." With a to-go cup from The Beanery

in hand, Amy strolled next to Lexi on Main Street's sidewalk.

"What are you talking about?" Lexi gave her a sideways stare full of skepticism. "I'm sure you did not mess up."

They waited for traffic to clear then crossed the street to Lexi's reception hall, otherwise known as the Department Store. Lexi unlocked the door and let them inside. They went up the grand staircase to her office, and Amy promptly fell into one of the plush seats opposite Lexi's desk.

She loved this space. Lexi was a wedding planner, and her office reflected it. Feminine. Glamorous. With its dove grays and pale pinks, it instantly relaxed Amy. Sometimes it was nice to experience a contrast with her own colorful environment.

"Okay, spill." Lexi sat behind her desk, leaning in with her elbows wide and her hands clasped between them. "What happened that has you so worked up?"

"I may have freaked out on Nash this weekend."

Lexi's mouth formed an *o*.

"We've been getting along and, I don't know, I guess pretending the past didn't happen got to me or something, because all of a sudden he's sharing all these details of his childhood I knew nothing about, and I sympathized with him, Lexi. I truly felt bad for him."

"What's so terrible about that?"

Amy mindlessly turned her coffee cup in a circle on the desk. "I wanted him to feel bad for me. I don't know, maybe I resented that he didn't know how hard it was for me when he left. I wanted him to suffer. I lashed out at him."

"You're not vindictive." Lexi smoothed her long

brown hair behind her shoulder. "And even if you were, he deserved it."

Amy chewed the tip of her fingernail. "It's not my style. Whether he deserved it or not, doesn't matter."

"You have every right to tell him exactly how he made you feel."

"It felt self-indulgent."

Lexi sipped her coffee and regarded the wall for a moment. "Amy, I couldn't be more blessed to have you as a friend. You listen. You care. You always want the best for me. And I want the best for you, too."

"I know you do," she said softly, getting choked up.

"Confrontation and conflict are hard for you." She leaned back, steepling her fingers. "If you feel conflicted, then give it to God. But realize you were born with a peacemaking personality. In your quest to keep things peaceful, I hope you don't lose sight of your own needs."

She'd never thought about it, but Lexi was right. "I guess I am a peacemaker."

Lexi nodded.

"It's hard for me to tell someone they've hurt me."

"I know. But if someone really cares about you, they need to know so they can apologize and not do it again."

"I know you're right." And Amy did know. She'd spent years praying for God to get her heart right, to keep Him number one in her life. "But my motives were bad. And it backfired anyway."

"What do you mean?"

"My stupid mouth opened up and I blamed him for me not having a family."

"Oh." Lexi blinked rapidly, frowning. "I'm sorry. I didn't realize a family was so important to you right now."

Her best friend didn't realize she desperately wanted children? Amy slumped in the chair. "I guess I owe you an apology, too. I assumed you knew I wanted kids. Sometimes it physically hurts me to see pregnant moms or dads with toddlers on their shoulders."

"Oh, Amy, I understand. And you don't have to apologize. I want children, too."

"I know you do." Amy stood and moved to Lexi's large board with fabrics, quotes and pictures of flowers pinned to it. She gestured to the board. "I want this, too, Lexi." She spun to face her. "I want a beautiful wedding and a handsome husband and life as a couple."

Lexi brightened, snapping her fingers. "Well, you just need a groom. What about Clint's friends Wade and Marshall? They're both very cute, and I believe they're single."

Amy pretended to gag. "You're forgetting that while you were off at college, I was dating Nash. I know Wade and Marshall. Sure, they're good-looking, but they're not my type."

"Well, Nash is out, so that leaves..." Lexi snatched a piece of paper from her drawer and started writing on it. "What about Nick Warton?"

Dare Amy confide in Lexi what was on her mind?

"I'm not going out with Nick. Nash pulled me close to him on Saturday, and it brought back all these feelings and memories."

The pen fell out of Lexi's hand. "Did he kiss you?"

"No!"

"Did you want him to?"

Yes, oh, yes! Forgive me, Lord, but yes.

Lexi shook her head. "Don't answer. I can see in your eyes you wouldn't have minded if he'd leaned in and—"

"Okay, enough." Amy went back to the chair and snatched her coffee. "It was an illusion. I was in love with him once, but I'm over him. I won't let him break my heart again."

"You know the verse about the spirit being willing but the flesh being weak," Lexi said in a singsong way.

"Yeah, well, I've had years to toughen up both my spirit and flesh. Nash isn't a bad person. He has a lot of qualities I admire. But I'm not a twenty-one-year-old girl with stars in her eyes anymore."

"He still hasn't told you why he left?" Lexi asked.

"No. He wants to, but I don't want to hear it. Whatever it was doesn't matter. It's over. And it's inexcusable."

Lexi nodded. "I get what you're saying, but it might not hurt to hear him out. It could give you some closure."

"I don't think so." Amy couldn't take the chance that what he would tell her would either break her heart all over again or tear down her defenses. Either way, she'd be the loser. She hitched her chin toward the paper on the desk. "Who else is on your list?"

"You sure about this?"

"No. I'm not sure about anything." Nash flipped through the quote again and handed the stack of papers to Marshall. A local contractor had come out to assess the cost of constructing an indoor training arena and other necessary facilities. The price wasn't what was bothering Nash. The reason behind the project was. "I keep getting this nagging feeling about it. And when I pray, I don't feel any better."

"Praying never makes me feel better." Marshall rolled up the quote and slapped it against his other palm.

"But if something's bothering you, you should listen to your intuition."

"That's what I've been thinking. Come on, let's take a walk. I've got to stretch my legs."

"Won't Amy mind?" Marshall jerked his thumb toward the house, where Amy and Ruby were making something for the kitten. This was their usual Tuesday time.

"No. The farther away I am, the happier she is." Nash hustled toward the path leading to the creek.

"I thought you two had set aside your differences for Ruby's sake."

"We did. And then we had a fight a few nights ago, and we're back to square one." Man, his hips and back hurt today. His knee, too. *Push through, Bolton.*

Marshall jogged to catch up to him. "What did you fight about?"

"She blames me for her life not turning out the way she wanted."

"She said that?"

"Not exactly, but that's what she meant."

"She's still here, though." Marshall handed him the rolled-up quote as they strode next to each other. Nash shoved it in his back pocket, wincing. Marshall stopped. "It's the third time you've made that face since I've been here. You're still in pain. When are you going to call the trainer I told you about?"

"I don't need a trainer." Nash was tempted to stomp his foot. "I walked past the gym. Picked up a flyer. It's not for me."

"Since when is working out not for you?"

"Since I saw yoga on the pamphlet. I'm not contorting these cranky bones into some weird pose. You might as well put me in a tutu and throw me on stage with ballerinas." The prairie grass rippled, reminding him to keep moving. "Come on."

"Every time you move, *I* wince. Your body is stiffer than a robot."

"I know, I know. What do you want me to do about it?"

"Make the appointment."

"Fine. I'll call him. You happy?" He glared sideways at Marshall, who was grinning like a doofus.

They continued in silence until they reached the creek. Sunlight danced off the surface, and the faint trickling of water running over the rocks filled the air.

"Marshall?" Nash bent to pick up a stone.

"What?"

"I think this is what's holding me back from making a decision."

"Wyoming?"

"No." He glared. "Training kids to ride bulls would be fun for me. I'd enjoy it. I know I would. But I don't know if I could live with myself if they ended up beat-up like me or, worse, disabled."

Marshall propped his cowboy boot on a boulder. "What's wrong with ending up like you?"

Nash could list sixty-five things about what was wrong with ending up like him, but he stuck to the relevant one. "I'm facing a lifetime of frozen muscles and creaky joints. I'm young, Marsh, and even you can see I get around like an old man. I got out of the sport before I was paralyzed or killed. How can I train anyone to ride bulls when I know what they'll be facing the rest of their lives?"

"I see your point." Marshall picked a long blade

of grass and wound it around his finger. "Maybe you need to ask yourself why you competed. You did it your whole life knowing the danger, dealing with the pain. Why?"

Punishment. Nash tossed the rock back into the water. "It was all I had. All I was good at."

"Did you ever worry about getting killed?"

Nash shrugged. "Not really." Was that true? Had he never worried about death? "I liked being number one. Seeing my name up there. I liked winning."

Marshall chuckled. "I think we all like winning."

Nash thought back to the other night when he'd held Amy and she'd lashed out at him. All he could think of was how much he wanted to get on a bull. Win or lose, every ride had been a challenge, a physical release. The only way he'd known how to escape.

He sighed. "What if I only did it to punish myself?"

"What do you mean? Quitting?"

"No, competing."

Marshall laughed. "Nope, not seeing it. You loved riding. You know you did. You had this gleam in your eye every time that chute opened."

"I did love it. But what's that saying about a fine line between love and hate?"

"Doesn't apply." Marshall shook his head. "Let me ask you something. Did you carry around a lot of guilt after you rode? Or did you feel all right inside?"

Nash had never felt guilty for riding whether he won or lost. "I felt all right."

"Well, there you go."

"But I also craved the danger, didn't mind the pain. What's that say about me?"

"I don't know, man, but I know your childhood stunk

as bad as mine. If you were punishing yourself, it was only a small part of why you rode or you wouldn't have kept winning. Ultimately, you had a gift and you used it. Be proud of that."

"What do you mean, I wouldn't have kept winning?"

Marshall stared at him hard. "If you had really wanted to punish yourself, you wouldn't have been careful, wouldn't have gotten to safety after each ride."

The impact of his words hit Nash hard. It was a sobering thought.

"So you're saying, my sense of self-preservation didn't allow me to truly punish myself?"

"Yeah. And what was there to punish, anyway? You're one of the best men I know." Marshall wiped his brow. "Has it been hard? Giving it up for Ruby?"

"No." He inspected a hole near the creek. "I was ready. And I'd give up just about anything for her."

"I know what you mean."

Nash studied him. Marshall's body bore witness to his daily workouts. He always moved with ease.

"Are the other bull riders in the same shape as you are? You know, in pain and having a hard time moving?"

Nash nodded. "Most of 'em."

"That's a shame. Too bad something can't be done to help them."

He could wish all he wanted, but his body would never be the same. And neither would the bodies of the other bull riders he'd hung out with over the years. At least he had money, this property and his little girl. Many of the retirees had no savings and nothing to fall back on.

Nash stretched his arms over his head. "Come on.

There are limits to Amy's patience. We'd better get back."

If he could just find a way to get into Amy's good graces. He preferred their truce to the curt nod she'd given him earlier. Maybe he should apologize. For not thinking how his leaving would affect her. For not taking the blame for ruining her life. For not giving her the family she wanted. For leaving her and their dreams.

Forget apologizing. It would only make it worse. Someday she'd realize he'd done her a favor. Until then, he'd be smart to leave well enough alone.

Chapter Seven

❧

Where was the peach fabric with the butterflies? Amy was supposed to be at Nash's in five minutes. Yesterday, after the Memorial Day barbecue at her parents' house, she'd planned today's project for Ruby, but she hadn't had time to pack a bag with the supplies. At this rate, she'd never get to their Tuesday craft session. She gave up on the shelves and started searching through the bins in the closet.

The time had come to talk with Nash about spending time alone with Ruby. The girl was comfortable with her. She no longer flinched when Nash stepped outside, and she even hugged Amy every time they were together. Yes, Amy would mention it to him later.

Her cell phone rang. She didn't recognize the number but answered it anyway.

"Amy Deerson?"

"Yes?" A shade of peach caught her eye. She dug the fabric out of the bin.

"This is Louis Whitaker with Orchard Creek Mills. We've reviewed your fabric portfolio, and I have to say, we're quite impressed. Are your designs still available?"

The material slipped out of her fingers to the floor. Her pulse started racing so quickly her vessels might burst. "Yes, they are."

"We'd like to offer you a licensing contract."

A contract! Her head spun. *It's happening!* All the beautiful fabrics she'd designed would be folded and stocked in her store. How many times had she searched for the right pattern and been disappointed? How many times had she wanted to make quilts out of her personal designs? All the years of learning Photoshop, taking online design classes, blogging and creating quilt patterns were about to pay off.

"...my assistant will email you the contract. It's a rather tight turnaround. We'd like to have the final design files in July to have the production ready for next May's International Quilt Market trade show."

July. It would give her a month to make requested design changes. She wanted to jump up and down and scream, but instead she composed herself and asked Mr. Whitaker the questions that came to mind. After talking for several minutes, she agreed to review the contract and promised to call him with any questions before hanging up.

Tossing the phone on the table, she leaped in the air and shouted. Her arms were shaking. Her legs were shaking. Even her toes were shaking. She shoved the fabric into the bag, grabbed her phone and ran out the door.

She called her mom as she hurried down the steps, told her the good news and promised to fill her in with all the details later. Then she drove to Nash's as a million wonderful thoughts tumbled through her mind.

As soon as she parked, she raced to his front door.

He opened it almost immediately, putting his finger to his lips. He came out onto the porch and closed the door behind him.

"What happened to you?" he asked. "You're smiling so big your teeth could blind someone."

"I sold my fabric line." She threw her arms in the air, and to her surprise, Nash caught her by the waist. She hugged him. Who cared if this was her ex? She wanted to celebrate.

"Yeehaw!" He lifted her off her feet easily, as if she were as light as Ruby. It was her turn to laugh when he spun her in a circle. "I knew you'd sell them. One of these days you'll have to show them to me."

"I will." Her eyes locked on his full lips so close to her face. He smelled good. His cologne should be outlawed. And then there was all that muscular power holding her so tenderly. Attraction made her lightheaded. His eyes deepened to almost turquoise and the pulse in his neck visibly quickened. A tiny thrill zinged her. She affected him, too.

"Will you stay in Sweet Dreams?" Nash asked.

"Why wouldn't I?" She eased out of his embrace.

"I don't know. I guess maybe you'd have to live in a big city now that you'll be a designer."

"No, I can do everything from home."

"You're sure? You won't be missing out on opportunities by staying here?"

Her happiness dipped a notch, and she stepped back. "I'm sure I've missed out on opportunities, but in my mind, you make the best of life wherever you are."

"You've never thought about living somewhere else?"

Did he want her to leave or what? "Sure, I've thought

about it a time or two. Denver is a fun place, and Salt Lake City is so beautiful."

"Why didn't you go?" His eyes gleamed with something she couldn't put her finger on.

"I think the better question would be why. I had no reason to leave." All this moving talk was killing her mood. "Where's Ruby?"

"She fell asleep. Has a low fever. I called the doctor's office and they told me to give her some children's medicine."

"Oh, no. Poor baby. I hope it's nothing major."

"I hope not, as well. Probably too much excitement at the fair this weekend." His voice was thicker than normal, and he kept tapping his thigh as if he couldn't stand still. "I'm really happy for you, Amy."

She detected a vulnerability she'd rarely seen in him. Normally, she'd leave if Ruby wasn't around, but she gestured to the rocking chairs. "Mind if I stay a minute?"

"I'd like it if you did."

Once they'd both taken a seat, she angled the chair to see him better. She fought for the right words. Lexi's advice about getting closure kept coming back. *Lord, I didn't plan this, but I feel like it's time. Should I ask him?* A sense of peace quieted her mind.

"I'm ready," she said. "I want to know why you left."

"Oh." He gripped the arms of the rocking chair and stared ahead before turning back to her. "Are you sure?"

"I'm sure." But worries returned. How bad would it be? Had he left her for another woman? Or had he fallen out of love and been unable to say it? He could have gotten bored with their ideas for the future. Or, like her mom had said, maybe being a star was more exciting to him.

"My mother got out of prison when I was almost twenty. You and I were already dating."

Amy's mind raced with questions. What did his mom have to do with him leaving?

"She had a nasty habit of threatening me if I didn't do what she wanted. She'd used me my entire life. When I was eight, I'd found a starving dog and told her I'd take care of it and pay to feed it, that she'd never have to do a thing. She let me keep it. Now, I won't tell you how I got the money to pay for its food—I'm not proud of my life back then—but I loved Digger. Several months later, she was on a cocaine binge. She was scary when she used cocaine. Thought she saw clowns in the walls. And that wasn't the worst of it."

Amy stopped rocking and concentrated on Nash's face. What he was describing brought a sick feeling to her stomach.

"She told me if I didn't shut Digger up I'd never see him again. Digger wasn't even barking. I hid the dog as best I could, but the next day he was gone. She made good on her threat. I never saw him again." Bleakness washed over his face.

"I'm so sorry, Nash." And she was. To lose a beloved pet must have been horrible.

"Yeah, well, that was life with dear old Mom. So, like I said, she got out of prison. Hadn't seen her or talked to her in seven years. I was already on the PBR tour. You and I were making plans for the future. I was happy. Life was finally going my way."

Amy had a sinking sensation, and she couldn't look away from Nash if she tried.

"But she found me. She always found me. I was out of town, getting ready to compete. She wanted money. A lot of money. I told her no way. She threatened me. I laughed. I was used to her demands, and there was no way I was caving. But then she threatened you. She told me exactly who owed her favors. They were dangerous people. It took me a split second to make a decision. I told her we'd broken up. That I didn't have room for a girl and a career. I wrote her a check for ten thousand dollars. Told her it was the last money she'd ever get from me and if she ever contacted me again, I'd make sure she went back to jail for good. I never saw or heard from her after that."

She hadn't expected his explanation. Questions popped up one after the other.

"If she left you alone after that, why didn't you just give her the money and come back here? We could have stayed together."

He steepled his hands together and brought the tips of his fingers to his chin. "She would have always threatened you. She would have hurt you."

"But—"

"Without you, she had no leverage. She could harass me all she wanted, and it wouldn't have mattered. She'd only ever been able to get her way with me by terrorizing something I loved. I had to make her believe I didn't love you."

Amy stalked to the porch rail, trying to make sense of what he was saying. She pivoted to him. "You don't know for sure she would have hurt me."

"I couldn't take that chance."

None of this was giving her closure. She was just supposed to accept that he'd left...to what? Protect her?

"You should have told me."

He rose, too, and moved a few feet away. "No. I couldn't have. I had to make her believe we were over."

"By making sure we truly were over? I don't see how either of us could have won in your scenario." So he'd dumped her to protect her from his mother. And he hadn't told her the reason because…? That was the key Amy couldn't figure out. "Why didn't you at least say goodbye?"

"For all I knew, she had one of those druggie thugs hanging around Sweet Dreams, scoping it out. She knew too much about you, Amy. Things she only could have known if she was spying on you."

Amy let out a dry laugh. "You make it sound like she was some sort of CIA agent. From what you've told me, I find it hard to believe she had such a master criminal mind."

"She was smart, attractive and manipulative. How do you think she kept getting released? Or regained custody of me so many times? She told her parole officers and the courts what they wanted to hear. You'd be surprised at what people will do to get what they want."

"Then I guess you didn't want me all that much." She shivered, rubbing her arms. His excuse felt flimsy.

He crossed over to her, his body inches from hers. "How can you say that? I loved you."

"Not enough, apparently." She stood her ground.

"She would have hurt you."

"If you would have trusted me—"

"Trusted you? I trusted you."

"No," she said, shaking her head, the reality of what he'd told her finally making sense, "you didn't. You never even told me about your mother. I would have understood, Nash. And there were other ways we could have handled her threats."

"You say that now, but—"

"It's okay." She put her hand up, a sense of acceptance washing away the hurt. He might think he'd been noble, and she didn't have to convince him otherwise. In a way, she was glad to know the truth. She'd always wanted a man who loved her enough to fight for her.

Nash hadn't been that man.

He'd set his own terms with his mother, and Amy had been the payment. Pain shot through her temple. "It was long ago. We were both young, and our lives headed in the directions they were supposed to go. We clearly weren't meant for each other."

"You were everything to me." He gently took her by the biceps, intensity blazing from his eyes. "I loved you."

"Love doesn't walk away and never look back." She shimmied out of his grasp. "Listen, I've got to go. I think Ruby is ready to spend some time alone with me. Tell her I hope she feels better. You can bring her over to my apartment Thursday. We'll try an hour by ourselves."

With stiff movements, she strode to her car. As she drove away, she could see Nash in her rearview mirror. He was leaning against the porch rail watching her.

All her earlier excitement from selling her fabric line disappeared. She didn't want to go to her parents' house. She didn't want to think about Nash and his psycho mother.

She didn't know what she wanted.

Rewinding the clock ten years wasn't an option.

She'd do what she'd always done. Move forward. One step at a time.

* * *

As soon as the dust from Amy's tires had settled, Nash did the only thing he could—saddled up and headed out. With his walkie-talkie clipped to his belt, he rode Crank up and down the pasture fence, staying close enough to the house that if Ruby woke, he could be back in a flash.

Amy had rattled him. The fool woman didn't know what she was talking about. She'd made it sound so easy: "You could have told me. You didn't trust me."

Bah! He'd trusted her. How could he have told her his mom was alive and one of the worst human beings on the planet? *Oh, by the way, Amy, while I'm out traveling every other week of the year, you might want to watch out for some scary men who might mess you up. My mother's drug buddies will do anything for crack and heroin. See you next Monday.* He couldn't have. She was wrong.

He'd thought about quitting the tour. Staying in Sweet Dreams and getting a job. Keeping an eye on Amy every minute. Every day. But his experience had told him it wouldn't be enough. It would never be enough where his mother was concerned.

He'd told Amy about the summers with Hank, but he hadn't told her about the rest of the year, when he'd been at the mercy of his mother and her other boyfriends. He'd learned at an early age to hide when they were using. If he didn't…

He wasn't rehashing the terror of those days. No sense going back.

The wind whistled as Crank trotted along. What had Nash expected? That Amy would listen to his reasons and forgive him? Thank him for putting her safety first? He wasn't that dumb.

Still, it stung for her to accuse him of not trusting her.

And now she wanted to be with Ruby alone.

He nudged Crank to go faster. He'd been soaking up Amy's presence for weeks, and it had soothed him like the balm he applied to his sore muscles after a competition. And now she was taking it from him.

From him? He scoffed. It had never been for him. She'd only been around for Ruby. But he'd sopped up her kindness, conveniently forgetting he could never have her. Maybe a small part of him had hoped she'd forgive him if she knew the whole story.

Well, at least he knew for sure she'd never forgive him.

The blue skies and sunshine gave the appearance of a perfect day. The rest of his horses were grazing in the distance, their tails flicking leisurely. He wished he could be like them, not a care in the world. Reluctantly, he turned Crank to head back to the barn.

The agitation spiraling up his torso wouldn't go away. If he didn't have bull riding to channel his restless energy and there was no Amy around to soothe his rough spots, how was he going to handle the unwanted pressure inside him?

Lord, I don't know how to do this. I feel like a balloon about to pop. But I can't get on a bull and take a beating anymore. Being in Amy's presence—even when I wasn't talking to her—made my anxieties vanish. And now I won't have her around either. What do I do? How can I shake this—whatever it is—that's weighing me down?

What was weighing him down? Shaking him up like a can full of fizz was more like it.

He thought of Hank. The drinking. The gambling. Hank's way of escaping his pressures.

God, I can't go Hank's route, and I don't want to. I've got Ruby. I can't end up drunk, broke and dead.

The words the pastor spoke every Sunday came to him like the dry breeze. *And the peace that surpasses all understanding will guard your hearts and minds in Christ Jesus.*

Exactly what he needed—a peace that surpassed all understanding. *Lord Jesus, please have mercy on me and give me Your peace.*

He relaxed into Crank's easy stride. The trainer Marshall kept hounding him to call came to mind. Would it really be that bad to at least talk to the guy?

He didn't want the town gawking at him. If the trainer wanted him to do sprints or something, everyone would see his clunky movements. What if his shoulder popped out lifting weights, the way it had so many times when he was competing?

He didn't want to fail.

Because if he did, running away wasn't an option. Not this time.

Maybe he was a coward.

Wiping his forehead, his thoughts zoomed right back to Amy.

He didn't blame her for being mad, for her accusations. Not really. He should have called and broken up with her. He shouldn't have left without a goodbye. At the time his decision made sense. It still made sense. Sort of. But she'd deserved better. Still deserved better than a beaten-up scaredy-cat like him.

His last memory of her from before he left was standing under a full moon in the driveway of her parents' house. She'd given him a wide smile as she stole his cowboy hat and placed it on top of her head. He'd yanked her to him, kissing her thoroughly. He'd been thinking, *One more week and we'll be engaged.* He'd just had to get through one more classic…

No more regrets, Bolton. You made choices you have to live with.

The sad truth was if he had broken up with Amy, he might have gotten over her.

And even he wasn't stupid enough to claim he was over her.

He couldn't go back, but he could make new choices. Better ones.

Chapter Eight

The following Tuesday afternoon, Amy uploaded pictures for her weekly blog post. Nash was dropping Ruby off soon. Their first girl-time without him. Ruby's fever hadn't broken until Sunday, so they'd had to skip their usual Thursday and Saturday dates. It had given Amy time to finish the rust, cream and navy quilt. She'd also reviewed the fabric licensing contract, talked to a lawyer, signed the papers and sent them off. Her parents had celebrated with her by grilling steaks. The evening had been lovely, but she was willing to admit, at least to herself, it would have been even better if Nash and Ruby had been there, too.

She hadn't allowed herself to dwell on Nash's confession. He'd done what he'd felt he needed to do all those years ago, and she'd been honest when she'd said they clearly weren't meant for each other. If the past decade had taught her anything, it was that she deserved someone who loved her enough to stick around and share his life with her. At least Lexi had been right—Nash's honesty had given her some closure.

A knock came from the door. She hurried to it, opening her arms wide as Ruby walked inside.

"I'm so glad you're here. I have something really fun planned for us today."

Ruby ran into Amy's arms. What a welcome! Amy savored her embrace. Nash hung back, adjusting the collar of his T-shirt with Eight Seconds scrawled across the chest. He wore basketball shorts and running shoes. Gone was his cowboy hat, and in its place, a baseball cap. Since he'd returned, she'd yet to see him in anything but cowboy boots and jeans. Unfortunately, he looked amazing no matter what he wore.

"Come in." She waved him in, determined to treat him like any other friend in town. Tension wasn't good for Ruby. Or for her. "Want to see my fabric designs?"

He gave her a sheepish smile and took off his hat. The man was too handsome. She led him to the wire where she'd clipped printouts of her designs. The pattern was off on one, and she needed to fix the color layers of another. She made a mental note to fix them later and flourished her hand. "Ta-da."

"They're paper." He sounded surprised. "I didn't realize they weren't actual fabric."

Her friends had said the same thing, so it didn't bother her. "I sketch the early ideas, then I take pictures and edit them in digital imaging software. That's where I add the colors and make each drawing the best it can be."

Was her best good enough, though? What if Mr. Whitaker didn't like the final designs?

She'd heard of other designers signing licenses and not having their fabrics printed. She was *this close* to having her dream come true—it would be devastating for the deal to fall through.

He peered at the one inspired by Indian paintbrush. She loved the pattern. The background was tan like the dry earth, while the red flowers and green stems repeated. The collection revolved around the colors of the Bighorn Basin.

"Makes me feel like I'm out riding the land. These are incredible, Amy."

And just like that, her treat-him-like-any-other-friend-in-town idea vanished, replaced by something more than friendly. His opinion mattered to her, whether she wanted it to or not. "Thank you."

"Miss Amy, what's that?" Ruby tugged on her arm, pointing to the print with whimsical animals.

"That is my version of pronghorns. Do you like them? They're like fast deer. They leap in herds around the countryside."

"They're cute."

"And so are you." Amy bent, touching the tip of Ruby's nose. Then she addressed Nash. "Do you want to stay for a minute? I made blueberry scones. I can put a pot of coffee on."

He continued to study each printout but glanced over his shoulder. "No, I've got a meeting with a trainer. But thank you."

Good. This is what she wanted. Time with Ruby. A cordial relationship with Nash. Nothing more.

She shouldn't feel let down, but she did.

"Well, RuRu, I'll be two blocks over at the gym. If you need me or start feeling scared, you girls can text me, and I'll come right back, okay?"

"I won't be scared, Daddy."

He met Amy's eyes over Ruby's head. He looked skeptical. She smiled to reassure him. Then she walked him to the door, and he lingered a moment with his cap in his hands. Was he going to say something? If he was, he must have thought better of it, because he just nodded to her and left.

"Okay, Ruby, do you want a little snack first or should we start our project?"

"Snack!"

"Good plan. Come and see my place." The living area, kitchen and studio were all one large room. She took Ruby around and showed her the fabrics, her art space, the sewing machines and quilt racks. Ruby oohed and aahed over the containers of colored pencils, markers and various craft papers. They ended up in the kitchen. After uncovering a plate of scones and cookies, she poured glasses of milk for Ruby and herself. "How is Fluffy?"

Ruby took a bite of a chocolate chip cookie. "She's good. She purrs a lot. But her nails hurt."

"Her nails? You mean her claws?" Amy bit into a scone.

"Yeah. She scratched me yesterday." She flipped her arm over so Amy could see the skinny red welt on her forearm. "It hurt."

"It looks like it. I don't think she meant to hurt you, though."

"I told her she was naughty. I 'nored her after that."

"Well, she's only a kitten. She probably doesn't know any better."

"She should. I bleeded."

Amy fought back a smile. "Try to forgive her. And be patient. When she's older, she won't scratch as much."

"As much? I don't want her scratchin' at all."

"I don't want her to either, but she's your kitty now, so try to love her. She's never going to be perfect."

Ruby's eyes filled with tears, and she set her cookie down.

"What's wrong?" Amy asked. "Why are you upset?"

"If I would have been better, Mama wouldn't have left."

"Oh, honey." Amy lifted Ruby out of her chair and held her. Ruby twined her arms around her, letting her cheek fall against Amy's shoulder. Amy stroked her hair. "That's not true. Your mother had problems. None of them were your fault."

"I was a bad girl."

"You weren't a bad girl."

"I was. I made her leave."

Amy rose, still holding Ruby in her arms, and sat down on the couch. She settled Ruby sideways on her lap. "What happened to you and your mother was complicated. She took things that made her mind not think straight. And they made her die. Nothing you did could have changed it."

"Are you sure, Miss Amy?" Tears stained her cheeks, but the hope in her eyes was what stabbed Amy's heart.

The poor child blamed herself for her mother's death.

"I'm positive. And, listen, I know your daddy takes you to church and talks to you about Jesus, doesn't he?"

Ruby nodded.

"God loves you so much. There's nothing you can do that would make Him leave you."

"But I can't see Him."

"No one can." Amy chuckled, hugging her tightly.

"But it doesn't mean He's not there. Can you see the wind?"

"No."

"Does it mean it's not there?"

"No."

"Even if you're all alone, God's still there. He loves you. And you don't have to be perfect. You can make mistakes. God still loves you. He'll never leave you. Even if you do the naughtiest thing ever, He still loves you and won't leave you."

"Are you sure?"

"Yes."

"I love you, Miss Amy."

Amy's throat knotted. The trust and love of this little girl felt precious.

"I love you, too, Ruby."

Bare Bones Gym lived up to its name. Nash kept his phone in his pocket while he waited for the trainer. Wide planks of wood lined the walls, and the high ceilings showed exposed steel beams painted black. The air was cool but it smelled like a gym—sweaty and raw. Nash didn't mind the ambience at all. His kind of place. He checked his phone. No texts or calls. Ruby must be doing okay with Amy. For the moment, anyway.

A dark-haired guy wearing sweatpants, running shoes, a form-fitting black T-shirt and a stopwatch around his neck approached. He had to be six foot two, and he was lean but cut. He stuck his hand out. "Shane Smith."

"Nash Bolton. Good to meet you." Shaking Shane's hand, he suddenly felt out of place. He was used to honing his body nature's way, on a horse or outdoors. This gym stuff… Could he keep up without making a fool of himself? Why had he listened to Marshall anyway?

"Let's go to my office. We can talk in private before hitting the floor."

Nash had trouble matching Shane's long, quick strides. By the time they reached the office, his left hip was flaring up. He gritted his teeth. *Never show the pain.*

"Take a seat." Shane sat behind a nondescript desk as Nash sat in the folding chair opposite him. "First of all, I'm honored you called. Your ride on Murgatroyd was like nothing I've ever seen."

"I appreciate that." Nash straightened. Maybe this place wasn't so bad. "Listen, before we go further, my four-year-old daughter is staying with a friend, and she isn't used to being without me. If I get a text, I might have to leave."

"No problem. I understand. I have a two-year-old myself." Shane leaned forward. "Now, let me tell you about one of my programs. I work with several retired rodeo men. They've all had severe injuries in the past they still suffer from. I don't know if that's your case as well, but I've developed workouts designed to lessen the pain and strengthen the weak areas. I call it Rodeo Rehab."

Rodeo Rehab? The name was catchy. If it lessened his pain and strengthened his weaknesses, he was signing up. Nash grinned. "Tell me more about it."

"The first step is the one every cowboy resists the most."

Nash bristled. He knew where this was going. The doctor.

"I recommend getting a full health checkup with your doctor."

"I've seen enough of them to last a lifetime."

Shane laughed. "I'm sure you have. But you were probably getting treated for an injury. I want you to have a full picture of what shape your body is in right now. Some breaks don't heal well, and physical therapy can make a big difference in your quality of life. I tailor your workout plan based on your overall health."

"I'm healthy. Healthy as a horse." He pounded his chest.

"That's what they all say." He raised one eyebrow. "I usually recommend weekly massages and low-impact exercises until your core is strong and your muscles flexible."

"Look, I've ridden horses and bulls since I was a tyke. My core is about as strong as it comes."

"I'll take your word for it, but you'll have to take my word on this—you aren't as flexible as you need to be. I can see it in your gait. If I had to guess, I'd say your hip's likely been shattered and never healed properly, and you've dislocated the left shoulder so many times, you can pop it in and out of its socket at will. I couldn't begin to guess how many times you took a hoof to the head."

This Shane was a good guesser.

Nash shifted in his seat. "You missed the broken ankle, collapsed lung, broken hand, dislocated jaw and torn ACL. Who cares? I'm done riding, so what's it matter now?"

"It matters because you don't have to live in an old man's body. If you follow my plan, you can have a much higher quality of life."

Nash blew out a breath. Sounded good, but it also sounded like a fantasy. Maybe this wasn't for him. He hated going to the doctor. All the lecturing and tsk-tsking irritated him. He prepared to stand.

"Don't you want to be in the best shape you can be for your little girl?"

He sat back down. Man, this Shane guy really was good.

"So...what?" Nash clenched his hands into fists. "I have to go to the doctor and get poked and prodded and lectured. Then you're saying I gotta have some therapist bending my legs every which way. Next you'll tell me I have to do yoga. I don't see any upside to this."

"You don't have to do yoga. But the former rodeo competitors I work with have seen tremendous results by strengthening their cores with Pilates exercises and yoga poses."

"You're killing me, Shane." Nash covered his face with his hands and ran them down his cheeks. "Absolutely killing me."

"I'm going to tell you what I told them. Give me three months." He held up three fingers. "If you're miserable and haven't seen results in three months, quit."

"Do we ever get to do real workouts? Like kick-boxing?"

"Have you tried Pilates or yoga?"

"No."

Shane grinned. "You're about to find out what a real workout looks like. Come on. We've got thirty minutes. I'll guide you through some beginner poses."

Half an hour later, Nash stumbled out of the building, feeling both energized and exhausted. His legs trembled from the poses he'd held. Downward facing dog? More like I'd rather climb a mountain with a one-hundred-pound calf on my shoulders. His stomach hurt from the planks. Even his arms felt like noodles after supporting his body weight in ways he'd never done before. But along with the pain came a sense of accomplishment.

He'd challenged his body in a very different way than when he used to climb on top of a bull. And the after-effect was similar—exhilaration, release.

Amy had never texted him, so Ruby must have been okay staying with her. Hope brought a spring to his step. He'd just worked out and liked it. He'd been able to leave his daughter with another adult for almost an hour. And, as much as he didn't want to, he was going to call a local doctor and get a full workup. He'd paid for Rodeo Rehab up front. He'd signed the three month commitment.

He just prayed it worked.

"It sounds as though she's really blossoming, Amy. I'm proud of you."

"I feel as if I'm the one who's blessed. She's such a dear." Amy powerwalked next to her mother around the high school track after supper that evening.

"That's another thing I love about you—your kindness. Didn't get it from me. You have your father to thank for that."

"What are you talking about? You're very kind. You do so much for the church and the folks at the senior center."

Her mom huffed, pumping her arms in the warm evening air. "That's different. I like doing those things."

"Just like I enjoy spending time with Ruby."

"I can see how you would. When I see her at church,

I just want to whisk the bitty thing into my arms and take her on a shopping spree. I miss those days when you were young. It would be fun to buy dolls and tea sets for a little girl again." Mom had a dreamy expression on. "Oh, I forgot to ask. How is the kitten? Is she loving it?"

"Oh, yeah, she adores Fluffy."

They kept their pace steady around the turn.

"So what's going on with you and Nash?"

"Nothing," Amy said truthfully. It was better that way. Even if her heart had been snagging and tripping every time he came to mind. His blazing eyes last week as he'd said, "I loved you," kept coming back, confusing her. "We had a heart-to-heart last week, and I think it gave us both closure."

"Uh-huh." Mom sounded skeptical.

"What? He told me more about his childhood, and I found out why he left town, and that was that."

"Oh, yeah? So why did he leave town?" Her mother's face was flushed. Amy was sure hers matched. They walked at a fast pace.

"It doesn't matter. I know. And he knows how I feel about it. Which is all that counts."

"How do you feel about it?"

She considered faking a leg cramp to avoid the endless questioning.

"I feel fine."

"Liar."

"Mom!"

"What? You're a terrible liar. Always have been. I'm glad. Means we raised you right. I know you're not fine with the reason he left. What I want to know is why." Her mom's tone took a diabolical turn.

Amy couldn't help it—she laughed. "Too bad. I might be a terrible liar, but I can keep a secret."

"True." Her mom waved offhandedly. "Another thing you didn't get from me."

They did another lap without speaking. Amy hadn't been able to concentrate on much of anything since Nash had picked up Ruby earlier. He'd said the workout had been tough but he hoped Shane's regimen would make him more limber.

She'd begun mentally putting together things she'd been ignoring. How he winced whenever he'd bend to kiss Ruby. The stiffness in his stride. He never complained about pain, so she'd assumed he wasn't in any. But she'd been wrong.

It was easy to believe he hadn't loved her enough to fight for her, but maybe she'd assumed incorrectly there, too. Maybe he'd spent a lifetime not complaining about the pain—any pain—physical or emotional.

And what did that assumption say about her? She'd believed he'd been happy with his fabulous life all these years. What if he *had* loved her the way he'd claimed?

Who cared? What kind of love did that? Just up and left?

Not the kind she wanted.

"Listen, Amy."

The hair on her arms rose. Mom only used those words when saying something Amy didn't want to hear.

"If you and Nash get to the point where you're getting feelings for each other, let me know. Dad and I will invite you all over for supper."

Amy almost stopped dead in her tracks. "What happened to 'that bull rider'?" She hadn't meant to say it, but she was curious.

"You're over thirty." Mom glanced her way. "I know you want a husband and kids. If Nash makes you happy, I want to support you this time. I'm still not sold on him, but, hey, I've been wrong before."

Amy had to blink away the sudden moisture behind her eyes. "Thanks, Mom."

"Keep praying, honey."

She'd never thought her mother would change her mind about him. Too bad it was for nothing. She didn't see her and Nash overcoming their past, especially since they were no longer spending time together.

It should make her happy. But all it did was make her sad. And as for praying…she hadn't been as regular about that, either. Between getting the fabric designs in shape, finishing up the quilt, spending time with Ruby and managing the store, she'd been spread thin.

But Mom was right. Prayer had always been her rock. She needed to make it a priority again. Trusting God's will had gotten her through the good times and the bad. She didn't have to do life alone. And she didn't want to.

Chapter Nine

"Ah, there he is." Big Bob waved for Nash to come to the back table at the diner Monday morning. "I heard you went to the gym."

"Where'd you hear that?" Nash slid into the booth, nodding to Jerry and Stan.

"Who do you think?" Big Bob held one hand up, hiding the fact he was pointing to Dottie with his finger.

"Dottie knows everything." He grinned. "I should have figured."

"Are you going to Bare Bones?" Jerry asked. "I don't even know if that Shane character can ride a horse. Never see him in normal clothes, neither. Does he own a Stetson or a pair of cowboy boots? Seems fishy to me."

"Well, fellas, I did go to Bare Bones, and I don't know if Shane owns normal clothes, but I do know this." Nash leaned in with his best conspirator's tone. "I'm pretty banged up."

Stan slapped the table and let out a belly laugh. "Son, we all are."

"Don't go speaking for me now, Stan." Jerry grimaced.

"You?" Stan said. "You're more bowlegged than a wishbone."

Jerry glared at him. The waitress slid Nash's usual breakfast on the table and poured a cup of coffee. With a wink, she sashayed off.

"Looks as though Trudy likes you, boy." Big Bob chuckled.

"She has good taste." Nash grinned before digging into his eggs.

"Hooie! Did you hear that? Good taste." Jerry laughed. "You are a handful, aren't you, Nash?"

If they only knew how tame his love life had been all this time. No girl had ever lived up to Amy, and he'd accepted his singleness. Well, until recently. Amy kept bringing life to feelings he'd thought dead, but he'd barely seen her since she'd claimed, "Love doesn't leave and never look back."

How would she know? He'd been looking back for ten years.

But his memories were as frail as plastic wrap and weren't enough anymore. He didn't want to look back. He wanted more of Amy today. Wanted access to those secret places in her soul she didn't let anyone into. But how could he get her to trust him?

He'd just have to learn more about her. Mentioning her name to these gossips would get him nowhere, though.

"When are you putting the training shed up?" Stan shifted in his seat.

Nash shrugged, taking another bite.

Jerry slurped his coffee. "Ain't you gonna teach those young bucks to ride?"

"I can't rightly say, Jerry." He spread strawberry jelly on his toast. "A part of me doesn't feel settled about it."

Big Bob considered him. "You're not competing anymore. What are you going to do about money?"

"I saved my earnings. Plus, I have my own line of chaps, boots and hats. I still get endorsement offers." But they would shrivel up as time passed. He wasn't naive about his status. New world champions got the endorsements.

The three men nodded.

"So you're looking more to fill your time, not so much to earn a living," Big Bob said.

He took a bite of toast, chewing it before answering. "That's right. I never turn down a paycheck, but I don't really need one at this point."

"I don't get it." Jerry shook his head. "You're plumb perfect to train the young 'uns around here. What's the matter? If it's a matter of bitin' off more'n you can chew, your mouth is probably a lot bigger'n you think."

Nash guffawed. "I haven't heard that one, Jerry. It's not that. My mouth is plenty big. I've spit more blood on the dirt than I have left in my body. Broken bones. Strained muscles. Had my head kicked in. I don't want these kids going in with stars in their eyes about the glamorous life."

"You could tell them about the dangers." Big Bob leveled a probing stare at him.

"But that's the problem. I don't want to discourage them, either." He sighed. "I don't know. I feel torn."

"You prayin' about it?" Big Bob asked.

"No."

"Well, get on your knees. You'll get an answer."

"What if I don't like the answer?"

"If it's God's will, you'll be okay with it. Eventually."

"A praying man is like a prairie dog…" Jerry started rambling on, but none of it made much sense.

When the waitress came around again and filled their cups, Big Bob caught Nash's eye. "You're in a position a lot of people dream about. Not worried about money. Time on your hands. So figure out what gets your engine revving. When you're excited about something and it won't let you go, you're on the right path."

What got his engine revving? Riding bulls and competing in rodeos had been his passion since meeting Hank. It had been the only thing he'd ever wanted to do or even considered doing.

Amy's words came back to him: "Then I guess you didn't want me all that much." In all the years since he'd left, he'd never once considered the possibility he'd wanted to ride bulls more than be with her.

He'd wanted her. Oh, how he'd wanted her.

But he *had* walked away without a word. And he had never let a kick in the head from a bull stop him from riding. So why had he abandoned Amy the second his mother entered the picture?

Fear gripped his chest remembering the evil look in her eyes. When she'd mentioned the men she'd send to "take care of" Amy, he'd become a young boy again, searching the streets for Digger. Watching helplessly as his mother snorted cocaine then disappeared for days on end. He still had the scar from one of her supposed boyfriends putting out a cigarette on his arm.

Shaking his head free from the thoughts, he picked up his mug. No more dwelling on it—he had other things to worry about, like his doctor's appointment this afternoon. Thankfully, Amy had offered to watch Ruby for him. He knew he wasn't going to like a single thing the doc was going to say, but if he wanted to continue Rodeo Rehab, he had to play along.

In the meantime, he was going to spend some time online and learn more about this quilting Amy was so good at.

"This one needs more sprinkles." Amy passed the container of pastel stars to Ruby. Nash was at a doctor's appointment, and she'd been glad to offer to watch Ruby for him. They were decorating cupcakes. She'd baked them last night after spending much needed time with her Bible and in prayer. Her studies had led her to Matthew 6:21: "For where your treasure is, there will your heart be also."

For the first time she considered the fact God might have been protecting her when Nash left. Not from his mom the way he claimed—but from Nash himself. His treasure clearly had been competing, not with her in Sweet Dreams. And she'd been spared from being second place in his heart.

The thought comforted her a bit.

"Is that enough?" Ruby placed several sprinkles on the frosting.

"Do *you* think it's enough?" Amy asked.

"More." She grabbed a small handful.

While Ruby continued to carefully decorate each cupcake, Amy's mind wandered. She'd barely seen Nash in a week. Strange—accepting that she'd been second place for him had softened her heart where he was concerned. They'd been a couple of kids when they'd dated. But they'd both matured. And she found herself missing him, wanting to spend time with Ruby *and* him again.

It wasn't as if she wanted to date him—although the

way he'd held her kept creeping into her thoughts—but she liked being in his company. Wouldn't mind being in it more.

Back when they'd met, he'd been thrilling, assertive and everything she'd thought she'd wanted. But the one thing she'd missed the most about him wasn't the thrilling or assertive parts—it was the easiness. He was easy to be with.

They'd always been comfortable in each other's presence. She'd been the accent color and he'd been the primary pattern in the quilt of their relationship. They'd complemented each other.

They still did. Maybe even more than before. He was solid and dependable where Ruby was concerned, but he also teased the girl and knew how to comfort her. And Amy was good at coaxing Ruby to enjoy the little things she'd missed in her neglected childhood, like tea parties and crafts and feeling safe.

She and Nash made a good team. For Ruby.

Not for each other.

She wanted to be the treasure in a man's life. Wanted to be where his heart was. She hadn't been Nash's priority before. Why would this time be any different?

If she could forget how his arms felt around her when he'd hugged her…

You're just lonely. It's been a bajillion years since you've dated anyone. Of course Nash would affect you. He's a very handsome man. With muscled forearms and not an ounce of give in his body. When was the last time any guy showed you some attention?

Several months. At least.

"Nice job, Ruby." Amy forced her attention back to the cupcakes. "Let's put them on a plate."

"When Daddy comes back, can we have a tea party?"

Hope zinged up her spine. A reason for the three of them to hang out. "Of course. We can even have it at the park if you'd like."

Ruby hopped off her chair and clapped her hands. "Yay! I love the park."

"Good. If your daddy is okay with it, we'll bring a few cupcakes and drinks with us. Why don't we pack up our goodies?"

Amy helped Ruby stash six cupcakes in a plastic container then handed her a stack of napkins and paper plates. They put bottled waters in a small cooler and tidied up the table and kitchen before washing their hands.

"Is it done?" Ruby wandered over to the rust, cream and navy quilt hanging on a rack. Amy loved how the patriotic piece had turned out.

"Almost." She took it off the rack and spread it out for her. "I'm going to wash it to make it super soft before I sell it. What do you think?"

Ruby pressed her cheek against the material, smiled and gave her a thumbs up.

She laughed. Seeing Ruby so enamored of the quilt gave her an idea. "Come here a minute." She led her to the shelves of folded fabrics. "If you were going to make a quilt, what colors would you use?"

A look of fear crossed her face.

"It's okay, Ruby. There isn't a wrong answer. I'm just curious."

Ruby tentatively approached the stacks. She pointed to a pastel pink fabric and a lilac one. A child's quilt with a kitten pattern would be darling in those colors.

"Those are very pretty. Can't go wrong with pink and

purple." Two raps on the door had them turning simultaneously. "Looks like your daddy's back."

Ruby raced to the door and threw it open. "We're going to the park and having cupcakes and you're coming, too!"

His eyebrows climbed up his forehead as he hauled her into his arms. "Is that so?"

"Yes."

He met Amy's eyes. "Is it all right with you?"

The consideration in his gaze warmed her. "Yes."

"Right now?" he asked.

Amy collected the cooler and tote bag. "We're ready."

"After you."

"How did you come up with lemon placemats?" Nash sat across from Amy at the picnic table. White frosting dotted Ruby's nose, and she was peeling back the paper from cupcake number two. He'd found Amy's blog earlier and, surprisingly, read several months' worth of posts. At first it had been to understand her better—what she did, how she earned her living—but her friendly writing style had sucked him in. He'd heard her voice in every word, and he'd gotten a better view of her world. It fascinated him.

Amy sputtered. "You read my blog?"

"Yeah. I enjoy it. Makes me want to sew a set of coasters."

"The coasters?" She gaped at him. "But that project was from October."

"Do they expire?" he teased.

"N-o-o," she said, skepticism all over her face. Her lightly tanned arms looked good against her royal blue

T-shirt. She wiped her hands with a napkin. "What were you doing reading my blog?"

He shrugged. "Guess I was curious." He wanted to admit it was more than curiosity. He'd spent almost two months in her presence, and the past two weeks of not being near her had taught him one thing. He missed her. He'd take whatever he could get, even if it was reading her quilting posts.

"Daddy, can I play on the playground?" Ruby pointed to the children's playset a few feet away.

"You sure can." He helped her get up from the picnic table. "We'll watch you from here."

Ruby trotted off and climbed the ladder to the slide. He waved to her as she went down.

"So, anyway, about your quilting projects…"

"Oh, you don't want to talk about those." She waved his interest away, laughing. "How did the doctor visit go?"

Frowning, he studied her. He never realized how much she deflected attention away from herself. Probably because he'd been so busy talking about himself. "You don't want to talk about the lemon placemats?"

Her cheeks turned pink. "Well, I can't imagine you want to."

"I do." And he did. He wanted to see her eyes sparkle the way they did when she enjoyed something.

"I don't know where to start." She rubbed her thumb and forefinger together. The gesture almost did him in. He wanted to hold her hand. Reassure her. But he couldn't.

"Start at the beginning," he said. "How did you get the idea?"

Her eyelashes fluttered. Then she peeked up at him.

"At my mom's. We were making lemon bars for a bridal shower, and one of the slices was so perfect. I thought bright yellow placemats with quilted sections to look like the inside of a lemon would be a fun project. The response has been great."

"I know. I saw all the pictures your readers shared in the comments. None looked as good as yours, though."

Her cheeks went from flushed to red. *Hmm.* Didn't she realize how talented she was?

"Thank you." Mindlessly, she drummed her fingertips on the table. "So what about you? Has it been hard, you know, retiring?"

"A little bit. I was injured pretty bad last year, and I knew it was time. Didn't want to admit it, but it got me thinking."

"What did you end up thinking?" Tendrils of hair blew around her face. Her lips curved into an encouraging smile.

That I had no idea what I was going to do and it terrified me.

"I've been trying to figure out what I'm going to do with my life."

She regarded him a moment. "And have you?"

"I'm working on it."

"I know this is none of my business, but seeing as how you went to the doctor…is your health okay?"

"Yeah. Nothing I didn't know, well, except for the arthritis." He scratched behind his ear. "Maybe the trainer in town—"

"Shane Smith?"

He inwardly growled. She seemed so pleased to know Shane. If the guy wasn't married with a kid, Nash might be jealous.

"Yeah, Shane. Well, he has this training program called Rodeo Rehab. I'm giving it a shot."

"I didn't realize he did that. What is Rodeo Rehab?"

"A lot of rodeo competitors are like me—stiff from repeated injuries that never fully healed. He developed a plan to improve our quality of life. I don't like some of his suggestions."

"But you're willing to try them?"

"I am."

"Good. I hope it helps. Maybe it will loosen your muscles."

"Maybe. I know it helped Shane's other clients. If it works, maybe more retired riders will sign up. About breaks my heart to see them hobbling to the competitions and rodeos." It was so easy to tell her things. He wasn't used to revealing his inner thoughts. But with Amy? It felt safe. "Can I run something by you?"

She nodded.

"I've been considering opening a training center for young bull riders. Giving them private lessons. But I don't know—"

"What a great idea!"

"You think so?"

"Yes, of course. Why? Don't you? You've got the skills, obviously. Is it the costs involved?"

"No, money isn't the problem. It's the danger."

Her lips twisted as she frowned. "Is this about Hank?"

He sat straighter. He'd never thought his indecision could be due to Hank. "I'm not following you."

"The gambling and drinking. His death." Her coffee-colored eyes captured him. He couldn't look away.

"The danger involved, for sure."

"You told me yourself kids are competing as young as six and seven."

"Some even younger. Not on bulls, of course. On sheep."

"So they're dealing with danger for years. No bull rider gets to your level unless he's done it his entire life."

The woman made sense. But what did it mean? He didn't know what to think.

"Maybe your heart isn't in it. You sounded more passionate about those retired riders hobbling around."

It wasn't that he was more passionate about it. Less fearful, perhaps? Maybe he needed to take Big Bob's advice and pray about it.

"Listen," Nash said. "I'm taking Ruby to the Dubois Friday Night Rodeo this week. Would you like to join us?"

She hesitated. He shouldn't have put her on the spot. She was busy, and she was already giving up so much of her time to help him. He just…well, he enjoyed being around her.

"Don't worry about it." He waved the idea away. "I know you're busy. How do you fit it all in, Amy?"

She crumpled the empty cupcake wrappers. "Fit what in?"

"The store, the quilts, the designs, the blog…us." He focused on her face, not wanting to miss her reaction.

She shrugged. "It's not hard."

"I imagine it is."

"I—" her eyes landed anywhere but his "—I guess I just do."

"Thank you."

"Daddy, Daddy." Ruby ran up, tugging on his sleeve. "Push me on the swing?"

"Sure." He stood, hitching his chin to Amy. "What about you? You need a push, too?"

He'd said it lightly, but he didn't move as he waited for her reply. Why did her answer feel so important?

"Why not?" Her bright smile did him in. Ruby raced ahead.

"I never told you I was sorry." He took her hand and turned to face her.

"For what?"

"For leaving you. For not saying goodbye. For never coming back."

"It's okay—"

"No, it's not. It's not okay. I'm sorry. I'll probably always be sorry. Anyway, thanks for letting Ruby and me into your life."

She looked stricken, frozen. *Great.* He'd made it worse. He should have let it go. They'd said everything they'd needed to say, and he knew better than to hope for a future with her.

He wanted her to know he'd regretted leaving her every day since he'd gone, but he couldn't admit it. Wouldn't be fair to her. He took a step toward the swings, but she stopped him.

"Nash?"

"Yes?"

"It was for the best." Her eyes shone with honesty. "God had plans for us. You would have been traveling on the circuit, and I would have wanted more than you being home for five days of the month. We both made the best of it."

Why her words tore into his gut, he couldn't say. Maybe because they were true.

He just wished it could have been different.

"If your offer still stands, I'd like to go to the rodeo with you and Ruby on Friday."

Amy turned the volume down on her favorite radio station later that night. She'd fixed the color layers of one of the designs and had settled onto her couch with a hot cup of tea. Why had she agreed to the rodeo with Nash? Shouldn't she be minimizing her time with him? Not latching on to any excuse to see him?

She couldn't even pretend she was going for Ruby's sake. She wasn't. And she hated the rodeo. Hadn't been to one since the last time she'd watched Nash perform. It had always set her on edge, worrying he'd get hurt or trampled. Ten years of not going to the rodeo had been great.

So why had she agreed?

The steaming water burned her tongue, and she set the delicate china cup and saucer on the coffee table. Was it too late to call Lexi? She checked the time. Almost eleven. Yep. Too late.

Face it, Amy, you like him.

She did. He'd been opening up to her about his past, showing her his vulnerable side. Then he'd read her blog and seemed genuinely interested. The fact he'd opened up to her about his uncertainties and asked for her thoughts about his plans made her like him even more. He cared about her opinion.

He couldn't be pretending, could he? *No.* When she'd sat across from him at the picnic table, he'd been looking at her as if *she* were the yummy cupcake rather than the ones on the table. Her heart fluttered just thinking about it.

No, stop doing this! He can't ride into town and get you back.

Did he even want her back?

She sobered up quickly. Well, he *had* apologized. And she'd needed to hear it. He'd sounded and acted sincere. So sincere she'd almost stepped into his arms and told him it was okay, none of it mattered.

But it did matter.

Rising, she pinched the bridge of her nose. Where had she put her Bible? She clearly needed some fire and brimstone. Anything to get her off these warm, fuzzy feelings that were messing with her head.

The leather-bound Bible lay on her nightstand. She grabbed it and returned to the living room. Where should she start? What book? What verse?

Closing her eyes, she searched her memory, but nothing came to mind. *Lord, what do I do? I've let go of my anger to the point I actually like this guy again. Worse, I could fall in love with him.*

Her eyes sprang open. What if she'd been in love with him this entire time and hadn't realized it? What if she'd never gotten over him in the first place?

Lord, I can't. I just can't. If I get close to him, he'll hurt me, and I've been hurt too much already.

Yawning, she set the Bible down and crept back to her bedroom. She didn't have the energy to figure life out tonight.

Chapter Ten

"Look at all the horsies, Daddy."

"Aren't they something, RuRu?" Nash carried Ruby on his hip. Amy strolled next to him as they headed toward the bleachers at the rodeo Friday night. The drive had been quiet. He'd tried to joke with her, but his humor had fallen flat. She must have added up all he'd told her about his health and his wishy-washy attitude concerning the future and found him wanting.

And why wouldn't she? He hated that his knee wouldn't bend all the way and he could barely run. As for career direction, he was no closer to a decision than before. Although, he had to admit, whenever he thought about the training center, he'd get the rush he'd enjoyed his entire life. But then doubts would creep in. And thinking of all the creaky old-timers would bring him back to reality. He still hadn't prayed about it.

"Mmm... I missed this smell." Lifting his nose to the wind, he inhaled. "Rodeo food. What I grew up on. What's your favorite rodeo snack, Amy?"

She darted a sideways glance to him. "I don't go to the rodeo."

"Ever?" He hadn't meant to sound so incredulous, but rodeo was a way of life in Wyoming. He found it hard to believe she never went.

"Ever."

Huh. And yet she'd come with him tonight.

"Why don't you like the rodeo, Miss Amy?" Ruby pointed to a small girl in a purple Western shirt and a black cowboy hat. "I like the white horsey over there."

"I do, too. Very pretty, Ruby." Amy's smile for the girl was so warm it could've baked a loaf of bread. "It's not that I don't like it. I don't know. I guess I've been too busy with other things."

Perfect. He'd taken the rodeo from her, too. She used to like it. Used to come to the local events and cheer him on. He'd missed seeing her in the stands. After he'd compete, he'd lift her in his arms for a victory kiss.

"Do you like it so far, Ruby?" Amy asked.

She nodded happily.

"Let's get something to eat," Nash said. "I see the Cheeseburgers in Paradise booth. Can't go wrong with anything on their menu."

They stopped at the rough-log structure and ordered burgers, fries and Cokes, then sat at a nearby picnic table and watched the crowd. The mountains behind them were glowing from the setting sun. Lights illuminated the arena next to them. An announcer made the audience laugh with his commentary on the kids' sheep riding event. Groups of elderly men in jeans, cowboy boots and straw hats leaned against the fence. Moms and dads could barely contain the energy of their little ones who'd been infected with the thrill of the summer night.

"Daddy, when's Uncle Wade bringing me a pony?"

A swipe of ketchup slashed Ruby's chin. Nash almost choked on his burger.

"Well, I don't rightly know if you're ready for a pony." He caught Amy's eyes, which were concerned to say the least. "I told him it was a big decision, and we'd have to think about it."

"I'm ready, Daddy." Her big eyes shone aquamarine in the pale light. "I've been helping with the horsies, just like you showed me."

"You've been a big helper, RuRu." Looking out at the crowd, he saw young children on full-size horses. He guessed a few of them would be barrel racing tonight. One girl couldn't have been much older than Ruby. "It might be time to get you riding, sweetheart. Are you sure you won't be scared?"

"I might be scared, but Miss Amy told me it's okay. When you're learning something you don't have to be good at first."

"That's right." Impressive. His little perfectionist might finally be willing to make a mistake or two. He nodded to Amy. "Thank you for teaching her that."

"I did say that, but isn't she a little young, Nash?"

He rubbed his chin. "Kids around here learn to ride about the time they learn to walk. If she's willing, I'm willing."

"But isn't it dangerous?" Amy studied Ruby with so much love and concern it almost took his breath away.

He covered her hand with his. "I won't let anything happen to her. I'll be there every second."

Her face cleared and she sighed. "I know you'll protect her."

"Can I pick the pony out?" Ruby asked, bouncing in her seat.

"We'll have to see. A small horse might be better for you. Ponies can be finicky. I want you to be safe. And we'll be going over a whole lot of rules and lessons before you get in a saddle."

"Okay!" Ruby threw her arms around Nash's neck and gave him a big kiss on the cheek.

He briefly considered buying her two horses after that sweet reaction. "You ready to watch some rodeo?"

"Yeah!"

He addressed Amy. "What about you? Are you ready to watch some rodeo?"

"As ready as I'll ever be."

He enjoyed her smile. For a brief moment he allowed himself to pretend they were a family. Just him and his smart, beautiful wife and their precious little girl. He could picture a baby in the mix. A little boy for Ruby to boss around.

These fantasies would be the death of him, but here, now, he couldn't stop them if he tried.

They threw away their trash and meandered toward the bleachers. This place reminded him of growing up. Of Hank and competing and racing around with the other kids. Of sweet-talking one of the food girls into giving him a couple of hot dogs and fries. Of sweltering nights in the camper and taking care of Hank's horses. Of getting in a chute, taking a deep breath and riding like his life depended on it because it did.

He slung his arm around Amy's shoulder and pulled her to his side. Whispered in her hair, "Come on. Let's see what these cowboys and cowgirls are made of."

Her scalp tingled where he'd whispered. Nash's arm was over her shoulder, and instead of pulling away, she'd continued her pace, pretending her heart wasn't beating as fast as the horse sprinting toward the next barrel. She'd had second, third and fourth thoughts about coming, and she'd barely said a word the entire ride here. But when Ruby asked for a pony and credited Amy with her willingness to take a risk? Amy stopped fighting it. She spiraled into their enthusiasm and threw her defenses to the wind.

Being at the rodeo with Nash and Ruby was the only place she wanted to be.

"Look at her, Daddy!" Ruby pointed to the teen girl flying by on the black horse. The girl's hair streamed behind her. "Can I have a hat like hers?"

"Well, yeah." Nash made it sound like it was a no-brainer. "We'll get you into full cowgirl gear next week. Make a trip to the Western store."

"I love the rodeo." Her matter-of-fact tone held a touch of awe.

"Me too, RuRu." He motioned for Amy to find a seat in the bleachers. She went up two rows and found a few empty spots.

"Is this okay?"

"Great." He smooshed in next to her. She was too aware of his masculine frame. The man radiated heat. She moved slightly to create space, but he filled it, too. Ruby sat on his lap, pointing to the horses every other second.

Amy tried to concentrate on the events. The announcer was quite funny. Everyone around them cheered and laughed and enjoyed themselves. As the minutes passed, she relaxed and stopped attempting to watch the riders.

What if she could have this all the time? Not the

rodeo so much, but Nash and Ruby? Having his strong arms around her? Being Ruby's mommy? Having kids of her own?

The idea was so lovely she allowed herself to dwell on it for a while. The chemistry was clearly still there between her and Nash. Ruby was the most darling child in the world. Nash wasn't moving away. He planned on being in Sweet Dreams forever. No career would rip him away, and neither would his mother. So why not fantasize?

Isn't this what she'd wanted her entire life?

She let the rightness of it wash over her and had no idea how much time passed. Events came and went, and she simply enjoyed being there.

"See that rider?" Nash nudged her, his warm breath on her cheek. A cowboy was running away from a bucking bull. "He needed to get centered before they opened the chute. And he wasn't jammed up."

"How can you tell?" Her voice was hoarse. What did "jammed up" mean?

"I just know."

The next bull rider was getting ready. Nash kept up a steady stream of commentary until the chute opened. "Come on, man, be a tiger!"

The guy's hand was in the air, back and forth, and then he hit the ground hard, scrambling away from the bull.

"He did better, but his back wasn't as into it as it should have been, and I'm guessing his shoulder was bothering him before the ride."

"How can you tell?" She didn't mean to sound like a parrot, but really, how did he know this stuff?

"I just know."

The sky had dimmed to the color of ink, and Ruby's eyes were sleepy as she settled into Nash's lap.

The next rider made it a few seconds before falling off, and the bull's hind foot clipped his arm. The man clutched it, his face in agony, as he ran off to the side.

"I could see that coming a mile away."

"What could he have done to stop it?" Amy asked. "Do you think his arm's broken?"

"Yes, it's broken, and there wasn't a thing he could have done to prevent it. That's riding bulls for you."

"I don't get why anyone would want to."

"Hank used to tell me, 'The only good reason to ride a bull is to meet a nurse.'"

She laughed. For someone torn about teaching kids bull riding, he certainly seemed to know his stuff. And he was so animated. So locked into the action down there. Didn't the man realize he'd be a fantastic teacher for any young competitor?

By the final event, Ruby was sound asleep on Nash's lap. He carried her as they followed the crowd to the parking lot. When they got to his truck, Amy stood by the passenger door, staring up at the constellations while he settled Ruby into her car seat.

"What are you staring at?" He stood next to her and craned his neck back.

"I was admiring the night sky. It's beautiful."

"I agree."

"Nash?" She shifted to face him. His arm brushed hers. Her skin tingled.

"What?"

"You'd be an excellent trainer for young bull riders."

"You think so?" He sounded surprised.

"Yeah, I do. You're passionate and you know what you're talking about. Your experience would help them."

"I don't know why it's been such a tough decision."

"Probably because you know the risks. And being there when Hank died… I'm sure it left a scar."

He didn't speak for a few seconds. "It did."

He shifted in front of her, then put his hands around her waist. Her breath caught. What was he doing? Please, let him be about to kiss her…

"I know I don't have the right, but I'm going to anyway. Blame it on the rodeo." He bent his head and kissed her.

His kiss was as good as she remembered. Better. It was like getting reacquainted. She wound her arms around his neck and kissed him back. This was more than she expected—it was powerful, right.

He ended the kiss, resting his forehead against hers. "You're mine, Amy. You've always been mine."

How could she argue with that?

But then reality splashed over her like a cold bucket of water. The rodeo was what tore them apart. She hadn't been his for a decade. So how could she stand here and let him wiggle back into her heart?

Years ago he'd followed the siren call of professional bull riding and blamed it on his mother.

What excuse would he use next time?

None. She'd fooled herself twice with guys who hadn't loved her. He could blame it on the rodeo, but she'd only have herself to blame if she gave into these feelings. Not this time.

"Nash?" She stepped out of his embrace, rubbing her bare forearms.

"Yes, darlin'?"

"Don't mess with my heart."

* * *

Like he'd ever mess with her heart. Nash kicked his feet up on the couch and took a swig of bottled water. It was one-thirty in the morning. He'd dropped Amy off a while ago, and he wasn't tired in the slightest. Annoyed? Yes. Restless? Uh-huh. Confused? Absolutely.

He couldn't be any more confused. The rodeo had kicked up all these emotions. He hadn't been away from the sport for this long in…ever. And he was tired of trying to convince himself riding bulls wasn't a part of him, like his lungs.

Rodeos and lungs—necessary for his survival.

When Amy told him he should teach the kids, that he'd be good for them, a weight had lifted from his shoulders. She had always gotten him in a way others didn't. Even *he* didn't get himself the way she did. So her advice was especially appreciated. And her insight into Hank had hit home, too. His death had left a hole.

Fact was, he missed the rodeo. Wanted to give young riders the tips and tools they needed to be successful. Big Bob had given him the high school rodeo coach's number. He could offer to assist the coach instead of starting his own business.

He'd spent his adult life responsible for one person—himself. Now he had Ruby. He didn't think it would be wise to add more people to the list. Maybe Amy was right about Hank. He'd never really thought about his death being part of his reluctance to open a training center. Seeing Hank die… He shook his head. Couldn't go there. Not tonight.

Frankly, he didn't know how he'd survived all those years riding bulls. All the chances he'd taken. The cautions he'd ignored. He'd been reckless. Only the grace of God had kept him alive and well.

And now Amy was in his life and it felt like a gift. A fleeting gift he couldn't hang onto.

Maybe he *had* messed with Amy's heart.

Who was he to fantasize about second chances and a family with her? Ten years ago he'd made the hardest decision of his life, and he hadn't looked back. No pining over "What if I hadn't left?" He'd done it. For her.

But what if he'd done it for himself?

She was right. He'd never told her about his mother. He'd kept his past from her. His childhood embarrassed him, made him feel like nothing. He'd been his mother's pawn.

Amy didn't seem to hold his past against him, but she was more elusive now. She had her own plans, her own dreams. She'd denied it, but all her fabric designing might take her to one of those places she'd mentioned—Salt Lake City or Denver. She'd said she never had a reason to leave Sweet Dreams before, but with her successful blog and stunning fabrics an opportunity could pop up.

One of these days she would put together all the pieces he told her about his past. She would come up with what he knew to be true—his scrappy childhood hadn't given him the foundation to be the kind of guy she deserved.

He'd already ruined her life once.

She deserved the best. And he was a far cry from that. No more messing with her heart.

Chapter Eleven

"Don't be mad at me." Lexi had just stopped by and was standing in front of Amy's freshly printed designs clipped to the wire. Last night's rodeo and Nash's kiss had kept her up until the wee morning hours. She'd tried to distract herself by fixing one last file.

"Why would I be mad at you?" Amy yawned, shutting down her laptop.

"I recently talked to my friend in Denver who is a buyer for a home furnishings company. I told her about your amazing designs and sent her a picture of the sample collage you gave me. Then I started thinking about it and realized that might have been a no-no since you signed a contract. Should I have kept the designs to myself?"

"Oh, no. Don't worry about it. If anything, you helped me. Orchard Creek Mills wants me to get my fabrics in front of as many people as possible. I'm sending them the final designs Monday. I'll be getting samples soon. Can you believe it?"

"I'm so happy for you!" Lexi hugged her.

"Want a glass of lemonade?"

"Sure."

Amy poured two tall glasses of lemonade and sat at the table.

"I'm putting out the feelers for potential guys for you." The way Lexi jutted her chin brought to mind espionage. Amy almost laughed.

"About that…" Amy drummed her fingernails on the table. "Let's put the mission on hold."

Lexi sprung to attention, her pretty eyes lighting up. "Why?"

"Well, last night…" She frowned, not sure how much to say. Would Lexi judge her for having feelings for Nash? Oh, for crying out loud, this was her best friend. If she couldn't trust Lexi, she had bigger problems than falling for her ex. "I went to the rodeo with Nash and Ruby."

"Oh, you did?" The words hung with too much hope.

"Uh-huh."

"And did you enjoy…the horses and such?" Lexi was clearly unsure how to proceed.

"I enjoyed the 'and such.' For sure."

She scooted forward. "Okay, I need details."

"The food was good. And I didn't want to, but I liked being with Nash…" Amy filled her in on Ruby's enthusiasm and Nash's pure joy and her own misgivings about getting too close to him.

Lexi nodded. "It sounds like you can't help it—you like him."

"I do."

"But you're worried about getting hurt again."

"I am."

"Does he act the same?" Lexi asked.

She squinted at the ceiling. "In some ways, he's the same. In others he's different."

"How so?"

"He's less brash. Humbler. Still confident as all get out, but he's more careful with people's feelings."

"Including yours?"

"Yes." Amy took a drink of lemonade. "He's actually interested in my quilts. He reads my blog."

"Really? Clint freezes every time I try to run a table setting by him. The man is terrified of fine china."

Amy laughed. "I know what you mean. When I dated Nash, he was caring and cocky, but he wasn't very interested in my day-to-day life. And I didn't expect him to be. But now that he's interested and actually asking me questions, well, I have to admit I like it."

"You should like it." Lexi nodded. "So have you two talked about the future? What does he want? I know you want marriage and kids. Does he feel the same?"

Amy shrugged. "I haven't asked him. I couldn't let myself go there."

"But if you have feelings for him…"

The pressure of his hands on her waist and his lips against hers rushed back.

"Well, you'll have to ask him what he wants, Amy. That's all there is to it."

She grimaced. "I don't know if I can."

"You're not a young chickie anymore. You're a successful businesswoman. It's okay to be clear about what you want. You can do this."

"What if I don't know what I want?"

Lexi opened her arms wide, a huge smile on her face. "Pray about it. You've given me that advice many times, and I can truly say it's the best thing you'll ever do."

"You're right. Thank you for listening and helping me. I'm kind of scared."

"Love is scary."

"Who said anything about love?" Amy tried to laugh it off, but the truth of it hit her. She could easily fall in love with Nash again.

"Not me. Nope. No mention of love here."

"I haven't shown you the surprise I'm making for Ruby." Amy padded to the table where she'd cut out all the pink and purple pieces of fabric for the kitten quilt. She'd already sewn one block. She brought it over to Lexi.

"Oh, Amy, it is adorable! And it's a surprise? Wow. I can't wait to see the look on her face when you give it to her."

"I know." She held the block out, imagining Ruby's delight when she presented the finished quilt to her. "It will take a while to make. I hope she loves it."

"She'll love it. She'll more than love it." Lexi checked her watch. "I've got to run. I'm meeting Clint at the deli. Let me know when you decide to have *the talk*. And I'll be praying for you."

Amy saw her to the door, said goodbye then collapsed on the couch. Excitement fizzed in her chest.

Her future. Nash. That kiss.

Ruby.

She covered her face with her hands. What had she gotten herself into?

Dear Lord, I need Your guidance. I agreed to help Ruby with the firm stance that I had to keep an emotional distance from Nash. And I'm failing. I have no idea what he wants. Last time I fell for him, I thought we were on the same page—that we both wanted mar-

riage and children. Lexi's right. I can't assume his future plans include both. But how do I ask him? I'm not ready to be in love, and I won't be with someone who doesn't share my goals.

Maybe she should stop this whole mess in its tracks. If she forgot about the kiss, pretended being with him was boring, told herself he wasn't really interested in her work…

Lord, scratch all that. Give me the courage to ask him what he wants.

If he didn't want a wife or more kids, she'd move on. Get over him. But if they were on the same page…

She had a lot to think about.

"Fluffy got so big, Miss Amy. Will you please come over and see her? Please?" Ruby clasped her hands and stared at Amy with big pleading eyes. They had finished their sundaes and were preparing to leave the church's Sunday afternoon ice cream social.

"How could I say no to that face?" Amy tweaked Ruby's cheek. "Of course I'll come see Fluffy." She glanced at Nash. "Unless you two had other plans?"

"No plans. Come on over. The cat is eating me out of house and home. It's positively plump."

"Fluffy's not plump. She's just…" Ruby searched for the right word.

"Fluffy?" Amy suggested. They all laughed.

"Hold my hand." Ruby took Amy's hand in hers, and their arms swung back and forth on the way to the parking lot. Amy savored the moment. The child had come so far from when she first met her, and Amy didn't take it for granted.

"Want to ride with us?" Nash opened the passenger door to his truck and helped Ruby up.

"I'll drive myself. See you there in a few." She got into her car and drove out of the lot.

She'd decided to pull up her big-girl pants and do what Lexi suggested. She was asking him the vital questions. About marriage. And more kids. And if he wanted them.

Her palms were sweaty.

What if he didn't want marriage or more kids?

What if he did?

Either way, she was terrified.

She turned down the country road leading to his house. The main thing she had to do was not let his answers affect her relationship with Ruby. The girl was too important to her. Amy wouldn't go back on her word that she was there for Ruby, not for Nash.

His long driveway came into view, and soon she rumbled down it and parked. He was just setting Ruby on the ground when Amy got out of her car.

"Come on, Miss Amy!" Ruby ran to her with her arms lifted, and Amy picked her up, giving her a kiss on the cheek. Oh, the preciousness of the girl.

"Where does Fluffy go when you're at church?"

"She curls up on my bed." Ruby fanned Amy's hair out as they walked to the porch. "She loves me."

"You're easy to love."

Ruby smiled.

As soon as they were inside, Ruby wiggled to be let down, and they went upstairs to see the cat. When Ruby burst into her room, Fluffy yawned, stretching out arms and legs before licking her paw.

"See?"

"She is bigger. My, my." Amy sat on the bed and petted the kitty. "She's still very soft."

They chatted about the cat for a few minutes before going downstairs to the kitchen.

"Miss Amy?" Ruby asked.

"Yes?"

"When I get my horsey, Daddy told me it will have a special stall. Can I show you it?" Ruby already had one hand on the patio door handle. Amy almost laughed at the excitement thrumming from her.

"Miss Amy might not want to go out there." Nash stood at the kitchen island.

"It's fine. The weather is so gorgeous I'll take any excuse to be outside."

"I'll join you, then."

Ruby opened the door and flew toward the barn. Nash matched Amy's pace.

"About the rodeo the other night…"

Her veins turned cold. Was he going to say it was a mistake? Or apologize for kissing her?

No, no, no!

"I appreciate you telling me to train the kids. You have a way of understanding me that no one else does. Not even myself."

She relaxed.

"It's obvious you're more than qualified, Nash. You should go for it." She wouldn't get a better lead-in. Question time. "Now that you're getting settled, how do you see the rest of your life going?"

His quick frown threw a shadow over his face. "What do you mean?"

"Well, I guess I'm talking about your personal life." Her voice sounded normal, but inside she was quaking.

"Hypothetically speaking, do you see yourself married?"

He slowed, staring at her. "I used to. I very much saw myself married."

She hadn't expected his answer. Couldn't look away from his eyes, more blue than green at this moment. "And now?"

"Not really something I've been able to consider."

What exactly did he mean by that? Normally, she'd wait until later to analyze his words and come up with a reasonable explanation, but not today. She'd stay on track. Get the answers she craved.

"Okay, assuming it *was* something you could consider, would you get married? Do you want more kids? Or is Ruby…" She fought for the right words. She didn't want to imply Ruby wasn't enough.

"If I had a wife, I would want more kids."

"That's good to know."

"What about you, Amy? Marriage? Kids?"

"Yes. Both." She peeked at him. He looked paler than he had a moment ago. "You don't look so good. Does the thought of marriage and more children scare you?"

He grinned, but it had no life behind it. "Me? Scared? I rode Murgatroyd, remember?"

Didn't answer her question. He might be on board with a wife and further kids, but neither seemed to have the same spot on the priority list as they did on hers.

"Miss Amy! Hurry up!" Ruby yelled, waving from the open barn door.

"Yes, ma'am!" She started jogging. At least she was perfectly clear how one of the Boltons felt about her. She wouldn't keep the sweetheart waiting.

* * *

What he wouldn't give for a chute, rosin and the meanest bull in the state. Nash paced outside of Shane's office Tuesday afternoon. They were going to review the doctor's results, and Shane would be laying out the first month's plan. Nash was ready for it. But he wasn't ready for all the other new stuff in his life.

All the changes were getting to him. No sooner had he adjusted to life with Ruby than Amy was back in it. And he'd tried to keep his heart occupied, but Amy filled every corner.

Why had she asked him about marriage and kids? He knew better than to think she meant with him. Yes, they got along well for Ruby's sake, but he didn't fool himself into thinking she'd ever take him back. The kiss the other night had been wishful thinking. Unfortunately, he couldn't forget the kiss.

"Don't mess with my heart," she had said. A clear warning she wasn't about to let him in it.

But then why had she asked him all those questions about a wife and family?

It had been all he could do not to picture her in a wedding dress.

Could he be wrong? Was she interested in him after all he'd put her through?

He'd always lived by the motto What Doesn't Kill You Makes You Stronger. And after every injury, every fall, he'd climbed right back onto the bull. He'd ridden whenever it was possible and even when it wasn't.

But love…second chances…

Had he lost his nerve?

Riding bulls day in and day out had been way easier than this.

"Come into my office, Nash." Shane rounded the corner. When Nash had taken a seat, Shane folded his hands on the desk. "How did the doctor's appointment go?"

"As expected. Bad knees. Early arthritis. Blood work is fine. Cholesterol's a bit high, but nothing to worry about."

"That's good." They discussed the particulars of his knees and arthritis for several minutes. "Are you willing to go to physical therapy?"

"I doubt there's much they can do."

"You'd be surprised."

"Well, I'll give it a go." He raised his eyebrows. "Anything a physical therapist can do for my hip? I've had three surgeries on it, and it's tight."

"Absolutely." Shane nodded. "We're going to keep your core strong while you start PT. Did your doctor refer you to a physical therapist?"

"He did."

"Make the appointment and get a regular schedule going. In the meantime, you can stand on the medicine ball."

"Medicine ball? Is this some hokeypokey remedy?"

"No, it's to improve your balance."

"My balance is fine."

Shane cocked his head. "Do I have to get out the contract you signed? Three months of doing it my way, remember?" He then went on about how core strength, balance and protective gear were helping up-and-coming rodeo competitors, as they made their way to the gym area.

Nash climbed onto the medicine ball. He fell off in fewer than three seconds. Frowning, he climbed right back on. And fell off. A fire started brewing inside him. If he could stay on a bull for eight measly seconds, surely he could stand on a dumb plastic ball for the same amount. Three more tries. Finally, he stayed on for almost ten seconds. He let out a whoop.

"We're going to keep building up your time each session." Shane gestured for him to get on the mat. "Okay, planks."

Thirty minutes later, Nash's limbs were jelly, and sweat stained his tee. For not running, kickboxing, doing jumping jacks or any other cardio, he sure felt beat. And Shane's comments about helping up-and-coming bull riders convinced him this was one of the pieces to training kids he'd been missing.

"Okay, Shane, I believe you. This, whatever it is you're having me do, is hard. I like hard. It looks as though I'll be opening a training center to teach young bull riders. I know you've got your hands full here, but I could use you, or someone like you, to get these kids in the shape they need to be. Don't get me wrong—I haven't met a teen rider who isn't compact and strong. I'm talking about the balance and reflexes. Getting their bodies prepared for the pain."

Shane was already nodding. "Count me in. I'd love to be part of any program that gives rodeo athletes the best chance to succeed while staying as healthy as possible."

"I'm guessing it will be a year before I can get everything running."

"It'll be here in Sweet Dreams?"

"Yes, sir. Right on my property. I've gotten quotes on the building. I just hadn't decided if I was going to go ahead with it."

"What changed your mind?"

Amy. Hearing her tell him he could do it, that he'd be good at it. Having someone believe in him, and not because he was a world champion, but because she knew him—the real him.

He shrugged. "Just feels right."

"I'm on board when you're ready to open. We can come up with a plan."

He shook Shane's hand, grabbed his water and headed to the door.

A plan. He hadn't had a plan in a decade. That one had blown up in his face. But his mother wasn't around to ruin this one. He'd give it a try.

Chapter Twelve

"You're becoming an old pro at using those scissors, Ruby." Amy crossed the room to let Nash in while Ruby cut out paper hearts at the craft table. Hopefully his session with Shane went well. She'd spent the morning putting the finishing touches on her files and sending them back to Orchard Creek Mills. She couldn't be more pleased with the end results. Opening the door, she waved him in. She returned to the table and nodded to the chair at the end. "Pull up a seat and join us."

"Look what I made, Daddy!" Ruby held up two misshapen pink hearts.

"Is one of them for me?" He rested his corded forearms on the table, and Amy had to look away at the sight. They reminded her of his arms around her Friday night.

Ruby's eyes sparkled as she nodded and gave him the biggest heart.

"Thank you, darlin'."

She picked up the scissors again and selected a baby blue sheet of construction paper. "I'm making one for Fluffy, too."

"Good idea. Here, make yourself a heart." Amy handed Nash a pair of scissors and a piece of paper as she addressed Ruby. "We can tie a long piece of yarn to it and you can drag it around for her to play with."

"Will she chase it?"

"Yes, and since it's paper, she'll probably scratch it up. So if you don't mind it getting ruined…"

Ruby's forehead furrowed. "I'll make two. One for scratchin' and one for good."

"Smart girl."

Nash was turning his paper like he had no idea what to do with it.

"Just draw something and start cutting." Amy shook her head. *Men.*

He set the scissors and paper aside. "I've decided to open the training center."

"You have? That's great, Nash!" Without thinking it through, she stood and put her arms around him in an awkward hug. He didn't get up, but he patted her on the back.

"Thanks. And Shane Smith's on board to plan their workouts. Want to keep the kids as healthy as possible."

"What a good idea. How long until you'll be able to open it?"

"Most likely a year."

"It will give you time to figure out all the particulars. This will be a nice way to pay it forward."

"'Pay it forward'? I'm not following."

"Hank trained you, taught you everything he knew about riding bulls, right?" She thought about the other things Hank did around him—the drinking and gambling. She chuckled. "Well, maybe don't pass on *every-thing* you saw and learned."

"That's it." He smacked his hand on the table, a big grin on his face.

Ruby flinched. "What's wrong, Daddy?"

"Nothing's wrong, RuRu. Miss Amy made me realize something. And I feel silly I didn't see it sooner."

She drew her eyebrows together. What was he talking about?

"It's not just the physical danger of getting on a bull the kids need to worry about." He leaned toward Amy. "It's the lifestyle."

Understanding dawned, and she straightened, nodding. "You can tell them about Hank."

"But not just the bad. The good, too. He cared about me."

"I know." She placed her hand over his and squeezed. His gaze met hers, and the thankfulness radiating from him made her heartbeat stutter.

"Who's Hank?" Ruby had resumed cutting the paper.

Nash's smile was soft and only for Amy. Heat rushed up her neck.

"Hank was like a father to me."

"But he wasn't your daddy?"

"Nope, but I loved him. He taught me about the rodeo."

Ruby got off her chair and climbed onto his lap. She rested her cheek on his chest. "I love you. I'm glad you're my daddy."

The picture they presented was so precious—Amy swiped her phone and took a photo. She doubted Nash had many pictures of the two of them. She'd text it to him later.

"Well, kiddo, it's time to rustle up some supper, don't you think?" Nash tweaked her nose.

Her bottom lip puffed out. "Already? I'm not done."

"You can take some paper with you." Amy selected several colors. "And I have plenty of safety scissors, so take a pair of those, too."

"What about the yarn for Fluffy?" Ruby began stacking her hearts.

"I'll find some." She measured out a length of yarn, snipped it and punched a hole in one of the blue hearts. She tied one end of the yarn to it. "There you go. Let me know how Fluffy likes it."

"I will." Ruby smiled, her eyes shining.

Amy saw them to the door, and Nash turned back to her. "I owe you, Amy."

"No, you don't."

"Yes, I do. For everything. Why don't you come over Friday night, and I'll grill some steaks? Unless you have a date or something."

A date? What was that supposed to mean? Was he messing with her? "Nash, I'm not dating anyone. I would have told you and Ruby if I was."

His face cleared. "Friday, then?"

"Sure."

He and Ruby left.

Strange. Did he really think she might be dating someone after asking him about his views on marriage and kids? She thought she'd been brave and made it obvious she was open to pursuing a relationship with him. Did she have to beat him over the head with it?

She frowned. Maybe they weren't on the same page after all.

Just like last time.

Wednesday morning Nash pulled on his boots while Ruby ate sugary cereal in the kitchen. Fluffy mewed up at her. Probably wanted some milk. Wade had just driven up, and Nash felt like a kid who'd won his first trophy. Ruby's horse had arrived, and it was a surprise for her. Funny how giving a surprise was even better than getting one. He couldn't wait to see her face when she saw the horse.

Too often lately, the face he couldn't get out of his mind was Amy's. He'd buried his feelings for her for ten years. He'd thought he was over her. Thought he could move back here and raise Ruby with only the occasional run-in and mild discomfort.

Yeah, right.

She'd hijacked his agenda—and his emotions. He valued her opinion, admired her compassion, craved her presence.

He wanted to kiss her again. All the time. Every morning. Every afternoon. Every night around sunset.

Lord, I'm about as dumb as a man can be. Help me get her off my mind.

"I've got to go out front for a minute, RuRu. I've got my walkie-talkie if you need me."

"'Kay, Daddy." She shoveled in another spoonful of cereal.

He hustled out the front door to Wade's truck and the horse trailer.

"Well, let's have a look-see." Nash rubbed his hands together as Wade rounded the back of the trailer.

"Ruby is going to love her. Gentle. Small. Older. The family I bought her from had three girls who learned to ride on her. Her name's Chantilly."

"Perfect." Nash clapped Wade on the shoulder. "Thanks, man. I always said you know horses better than anyone."

"Years of experience." He grinned. "If Ruby doesn't like her, give me a call. I have two other options."

"I don't think it will be an issue. The girl's horse crazy."

"My kind of girl."

"Mine, too." Nash chuckled. "Well, let's see the old gal."

Wade backed the horse out onto the gravel, then he stroked her back, speaking softly to her. She seemed right at home.

"She is a beauty." Nash whistled, slowly running his hand down her neck. "How did you know Ruby would want a white horse?"

"Just a coincidence." He led Chantilly toward the barn as they discussed her. When they reached the pasture fence, Wade asked, "Want to bring Ruby out?"

"You know I do. Be right back." He hurried to the patio and into the kitchen. "Get your shoes on. There's a surprise out front for you."

"What is it?" Worry lines creased her forehead.

"You're going to like it." He winked.

She scrambled to the mat where her shoes were kept and ran back to Nash. The picture she presented made him laugh—she wore a purple nightgown, her hair hadn't been brushed and her bare feet were shoved into tennis shoes with the laces trailing.

"Let's get those shoes tied before you trip and break a tooth." He crouched, ignoring his stiff joints, and tied her shoes before patting her on the head and following her outside.

When Ruby saw Wade and the white horse, she stopped in her tracks.

"Daddy, Uncle Wade has a horsey."

"I know."

Her face turned up to him with such longing Nash almost grabbed his chest.

"It's for you, RuRu. It's your horse." Once more, she was off and running. "Steer clear of its hind legs."

Circling wide around the animal, she came up to Wade and stood next to him. "Is it really mine, Uncle Wade?"

"Sure is, cutie." He grinned. "Meet Chantilly."

Nash joined them, patting the horse's neck.

Ruby lifted her arms to Wade, her face glowing with adoration, and Wade handed Nash the lead rope before picking her up. "What a mighty fine welcome, Ruby."

"A white horsey," she said, awestruck. "All mine!"

"We'll saddle her up for you, but not today. She needs a little time to get used to her new home first."

"I'll help Shalilly. I'll make sure she ain't lonely or scared."

"It's Chantilly," Nash said. "This horse is a big responsibility. You and I will be going over a lot of rules. And it might take time for her to trust you. Can you accept that?"

Wade set Ruby down, and she thought for a moment before nodding. "I understand, Daddy. Chantilly might think her mommy hated her and that's why she's here, but I'll tell her every day how much I love her."

Nash wasn't sure what to make of that comment. "This horse doesn't think her mommy hates her. In fact, she's old. She lived with three girls who all grew up riding her."

"They just threw her out?" Ruby's eyes filled with tears.

"No, they sold her to Uncle Wade. The girls all got

big and didn't have time to ride her anymore. She'll be very happy to have you taking care of her."

"I will. I'll love her and brush her and sing songs to her and read her stories…"

Wade met Nash's eyes and they both fought back laughter.

"You moved the horses to the new pasture, right?" Wade asked.

"Yes."

"Lead her around the fence line of the empty pasture and show her where the food is. The other horses will probably come up to the fence to check her out." Wade started walking backward toward his truck. "I'll get her feed and paperwork."

"You heard Uncle Wade." Nash looked at Ruby. "Let's take her around the pasture."

He held the lead rope while Ruby clutched his other hand, skipping next to him.

"I can't wait to tell Miss Amy I have my own horsey. She's going to love her. I'm going to tell Chantilly it's okay to feel sad sometimes, but Jesus is with her when she's missing her family. That's what Miss Amy told me, Daddy. And I'm going to tell Chantilly she'll always have lots of food here, and we'll never, ever leave her…"

Nash tried to keep up with Ruby's train of thought. The poor child's fears…based on her own rotten experience with their mother. He realized how much Ruby had blossomed with Amy around. A few months ago she'd barely talked, never smiled, shrank away from all physical contact, and here she was, sharing all the best things Amy taught her.

"Don't tell Miss Amy I have Chantilly, though, Daddy. I want to show her myself."

"You got it, RuRu."

"I love Miss Amy, Daddy."

I do, too.

His lungs locked up.

He loved Amy.

Still loved her. Had never stopped. And this time it was deeper, less selfish—and impossible. Absolutely impossible.

He frowned. Why? Didn't Ruby deserve to have a good mother, too? A mother like Amy?

Stop the wishful thinking!

Amy didn't want him messing with her heart. But she did want marriage and kids. What was he missing?

Had she been warning him?

Or warming up to him?

His throat felt like it was lined with sandpaper.

"I think Chantilly likes it here," Ruby said.

The horse seemed docile and sweet. When they'd taken her around the perimeter and showed her the feed station and water, they took the lead off her halter and let her settle in.

"We'll let her explore for a while." He tapped his finger against his chin. He had to run away from thinking about l-o-v-e all day. "You know what you need?"

She shook her head.

"If you're going to be a cowgirl, it's time to get you outfitted in cowboy boots, a hat and gear. I'll see if Uncle Wade wants to join us. Run up to your room and get dressed, okay?"

"Yay! Cowgirl clothes!"

"Tell Ruby I'm sorry I have to miss our craft time this afternoon, but I'll still be over tomorrow night."

Amy held her phone to her ear as she clicked open the digital files Orchard Creek Mills had emailed back to her. The repeating pattern was off slightly in one file, and another had a design element they found too fussy. They needed the files fixed and returned tomorrow.

"I'll tell her," he said. "Is everything all right?"

"Yes, it's fine." She filled him in about the files she needed to fix. "I've got to get this right for them. I have so many more ideas for fabrics, and I'm spending a ton of money to have a booth at the quilt trade show next year. I can't fail. I just can't fail at this. I want buyers to love my collection. It will open up so many doors."

"They'll love it. How could they not?"

His emotional support was like a much-needed hug. "Thank you, Nash. Listen, I've got to go. I'll be over tomorrow night."

"Hey, Amy?"

"Yeah?"

"Don't put too much pressure on yourself. Your best is good enough."

"Thanks." After hanging up, she tried to concentrate on the files, but Nash's words kept plucking at her heart.

While in theory she agreed with him, she struggled to apply it to herself. She strove to do her best—to be the best she could be—but it didn't always add up to her believing it.

She never really felt like she was good enough.

And these files brought out her insecurities.

What if she fixed everything, sent them back and Mr. Whitaker didn't like them? What if Orchard Creek Mills walked away from the contract? Until she had the fabrics in her hands, she couldn't be sure they would keep their word.

They like your work, Amy.

This excitement—this feeling of finally getting what she'd wanted after craving it for so long—was familiar. She'd had it right before Nash left town. She'd had the impression he wanted to propose. Then he had vanished. And later, when she got serious with John, she'd practically tasted the engagement ring, the wedding ceremony, the house in town, the kids.

And both times her hopes had been dashed so suddenly, she'd thought she would have a nervous breakdown.

Well, she'd come close to a breakdown after Nash.

She zoomed in on the file. Nash was wrong. Her best had never been good enough. That's why these drawings needed to be perfect. She'd give the company no reason to doubt working with her. None at all.

Chapter Thirteen

Tonight could change his life.

Nash smoothed his hands down the front of his new shirt and studied his appearance in the mirror. Not bad. And that was saying something. Ever since he'd realized he still loved Amy, he'd been a mess. He couldn't get her off his mind. He had to do something about it.

He just wasn't sure what.

He'd bought her flowers—a mixture of colorful blooms—picked out the thickest, juiciest steaks from the market, cleaned the house, bought *and lit* a scented candle and had even tossed a salad for them. Green leafy things didn't usually grace his plate, but this was for Amy. He'd endure fresh vegetables.

Should he admit he loved her and beg her to give him a second chance? Tell her he'd never let her down again? Shout that he'd changed, that he wasn't the same man who'd left her high and dry?

It all made him queasy.

He couldn't honestly say he'd never let her down again. And had he changed? He was the same old Nash. He couldn't bear to hurt her, but it wasn't as if he had the best track record of stepping up and doing the right thing. Maybe she was better off without him.

Lord, I need Your help. I don't know what to say or do, but I want to put Amy first this time.

"Daddy?" Ruby called from her room.

"What do you need?" he yelled back.

"I can't get my shirt buttoned."

"Be right there." He gave his appearance one more quick look. Good enough.

After helping Ruby button her new Western shirt— pink and white, naturally—he went out to the patio to fire up the grill. He turned the gas to medium-high and glanced through the patio door at Ruby. She was attempting to wrap a ribbon around Fluffy's neck. He went back inside before she strangled the poor thing.

"I can't get it on her, and Fluffy's being bad." Ruby threw the ribbon down and stomped her foot, clad in a pink cowboy boot.

"Cats don't like people tying 'em up, RuRu." He crouched down. "She's not being bad. Here, let me try it."

Ruby picked up the purple ribbon and gave it to him.

"You hold the fleabag while I tie it."

She held Fluffy while he got it around the wiggly kitten's neck, then loosely tied it in a bow.

"You did it, Daddy!" She set Fluffy down and hugged Nash. He held her tightly, enjoying how everything he did in her eyes was heroic. She pulled back, clapping her hands. "I can't wait to show Chantilly to Miss Amy!"

"I know you can't wait."

"Will you do the pigtails again?" Ruby held out two hair elastics. He'd watched a video on how to pull Ruby's hair into pigtails. He'd also watched a video on braiding, but it was beyond him at this point.

"You got it." He parted her hair and smoothed the sections to the side then fastened each into an elastic band. "You are the very picture of a cowgirl."

She grinned. A knock at the door propelled her into motion. "I'll get it!"

He wiped his sweaty palms down his jeans and willed himself to act normal.

"Hi!" Amy beamed, holding Ruby's hand, as she entered the kitchen. She wore a simple sundress and strappy sandals. Her hair tumbled around her tanned shoulders. She looked prettier than he'd ever seen her. His collar tightened around his neck. She gestured to Ruby's outfit. "I see you went shopping. Great choice."

"You like my boots, Miss Amy?" Ruby lifted her foot.

"I love them. I might have to get a matching pair. Then we could be twinsies."

"Twinsies!" Ruby's eyes widened. "What's that?"

"It's when two good friends dress the same. Like twins."

"Daddy, tell Miss Amy where we got the boots so she can get some just like mine."

"You are a vision tonight, Miss Amy." He met her eyes, all sparkling and brown, and his legs positively wobbled. "And as for the boots, the Western store in town will be sure to hook you up." His voice cracked on the last word. He mentally shook himself—*get it together!*

"Come on, I got a surprise!" Ruby tugged Amy's hand and dragged her to the patio.

"I'll throw the steaks on." Nash uncovered the plate of meat and found the tongs, but all he could think about was Amy in that dress.

"Okay," Amy said, "but then we need to come back in because I have something to tell your daddy."

Nash rubbed his chin, watching them stroll hand in hand to the barn. What did Amy want to tell him? Her hair waved in the breeze, and her shapely legs peeked out from under the dress. Ruby kept jumping up and turning to talk to Amy. Her patience amazed him.

He put the steaks on the grill, his mouth watering as the meat sizzled. The blue sky and hot temperature combined to make the ideal summer day. With these conditions, Ruby so happy and Amy shining like the brightest star, he'd be a fool not to tell her how he felt about her. The timing was right.

Sitting on the patio chair, he propped his ankle on his knee and breathed in the fresh air. Chantilly was still in a separate pasture, but the way she and the other horses kept checking each other out at the fence line, he figured she could join them in another day or two.

He'd called the contractor, and they'd agreed on a price and timeline to construct another barn, a new building with an indoor arena, locker rooms and additional parking space. A crew would be out next week to begin.

He flipped the steaks as Amy and Ruby approached.

"I'm going to find Fluffy. She has a bow on!" Ruby raced indoors, leaving him and Amy alone.

"Guess what?" Her red lips and big smile were blinding him. Whatever she had to say must be pretty great for her to be so happy. And if she was in a good mood now, didn't that bode well for him to declare his feelings?

"What?" He closed the grill to let the steaks cook a few more minutes.

"I got a call when I was heading out the door to come

here. It was the buyer for a home furnishings company. She wants to hire me!"

Hire her? Nash scratched his neck as dread washed over him. What was she talking about?

"Lexi planned this woman's wedding a few years ago, and, since they both lived in Denver at the time, they became friends. Lexi told her about my fabrics and texted her a few pictures. Apparently, she did an internet search and loved what she saw…"

Denver. The word repeated over and over in his mind. Amy liked Denver. Thought it was a fun town. She'd said herself she'd never had a reason to move.

And now she did.

He fought a drowning sensation. If she took the job, he couldn't follow her. Ruby was doing so well in Sweet Dreams. The therapist had drilled into him that she needed stability—a real home—long term. And he'd agreed. Promised himself he'd stick it out for Ruby. No matter what.

All the words he'd been ready to say stuck in his throat. He couldn't deny Amy this opportunity. She'd worked hard to get to this point. Just the other night she'd been so stressed about failing at this.

With the heaviest of hearts, he tuned back in to what she was saying.

"…pillows and furniture, but I never thought about doing that type of work."

He clenched his jaw, took a deep breath and looked her in the eye. "You should take the job."

"What?" Her nose scrunched, and she shook her head. "No, I don't want it."

"Denver is a great city, and you worked hard for this."

"I didn't work hard for *this*. I worked hard to have my own fabric line. Two different things."

"You'll regret it if you don't go." The words came out harsher than he intended. But the thought of her moving tore him up inside. He wanted to trap her here, make her stay, but he wouldn't be that selfish.

She crossed her arms over her chest and thrust her hip out. "Are you trying to get rid of me?"

Her excitement morphed into frustration. Why was he telling her to go? Didn't he have feelings for her? Or had the friendship they'd rebuilt been a sham?

"I want what's best for you." Nash stood next to the grill. Gone was the mischievous twinkle in his eyes. He looked like a tough cowboy who wouldn't budge.

"Well, I don't want the job." She hiked up her chin. "It was an ego boost to be asked, and, yeah, I'm flattered, but I don't want to move."

"It would be a step up."

"A step up from what? In case you haven't noticed, I run a successful quilt store right here in Sweet Dreams. I sell my patterns online, have a popular blog and now can add fabric designer to my credentials. I'm sorry you think what I've accomplished is a step down."

"That's not what I meant and you know it."

"No, I don't know it, Nash. I have no idea what you think. All I know is I've worked hard for a decade to get where I'm at, and I don't need anyone telling me what to do."

"I'm not telling you what to do."

"Yes, that's exactly what you're doing." She'd been growing close to him, and once again, he'd blindsided her. He acted as if he wanted her gone, out of Sweet Dreams, out of his life.

Didn't he understand Denver offered her nothing? Everything she wanted was right here.

Nash stood with his legs wide. "There are more opportunities for you there."

"'Opportunities'?" She huffed. "What about my loyal customers—many who have become good friends? I would lose more than I would gain—my store, my friends, my family."

"You don't lose your friends and family when you move. You'd still talk to them. You'd visit."

"It's not the same." Heaviness descended on her heart. With every word, he was pushing her to go. But why? If this was the end, she didn't want to spend the next ten years wondering what went wrong. She'd done that once. She wouldn't do it again. "What's going on, Nash? I thought we're growing close."

"We are." He averted his eyes.

"You kissed me."

"Yeah."

"Am I imagining the connection between us? We get along well. Always have."

"You're not imagining it." He licked his lips. "But I'm not going to stand in the way of the career you've worked hard for."

She wanted to scream. "But that's what I'm trying to tell you—I didn't work hard to move away and work for someone else."

"If you stay here, you'll regret it." His voice was cold.

"I know I'm regretting telling you about it." Her heart was shrinking. She didn't need to be hit over the head with what he was trying to tell her, but it hurt. Once again, she'd trusted him, and once again, he'd been the wrong guy to trust.

"Forget it." He turned away. "Do what you want."

Do what she wanted? She straightened, growing more disillusioned with each passing second. What was his deal? He'd been kind and open and easy to be with ever since he'd come back to town. She knew he was attracted to her and she guessed it was more than that, after she'd caught him staring at her and the kiss from the rodeo. It was love, wasn't it?

If this was love, why was he pushing her away?

Last time he ran away.

He couldn't run away this time. Not with Ruby in his care.

Was he trying to make her leave because he couldn't go anywhere himself?

Well, then whatever he felt for her wasn't enough.

It had never been enough.

Maybe his relationships with his mother and Hank had burned him to the point he wasn't capable of loving Amy the way she wanted to be loved.

"I know what you're doing," she said. "You're pushing me out of your life. You escaped to the rodeo before, but this time you can't. Well, guess what? I'm not Hank, who used you and got himself killed. And I'm certainly not your mother, who was completely unqualified to take care of herself, let alone raise two children. I'm trustworthy, Nash. But you still don't trust me." She pulled her shoulders back, tossed her hair. "If you want me out of your life, say so. You don't need to drive me away. I'll go and never come back."

"I do trust you." He hung his head. "But I'll only let you down."

He wasn't even willing to fight for her? Red-hot fury boiled in her veins. "Well, I guess we agree on something. All you've ever done is let me down!"

She couldn't stay another second. She ran across the patio through the yard to the driveway where her car was parked. With shaky breaths she tried to remember if she'd left her purse in the house, but no, it was sitting on the passenger seat. She got in, tried to calm her trembling fingers and jammed the key into the ignition. Checked her mirrors.

Nash had followed her. He stood to the side of her car. His face had paled. His eyes were filled with panic. He didn't move, didn't say anything, but his lips looked blue and his stillness was eerily familiar.

Don't think about it. Just go!

She backed up as Ruby, arms flailing, ran out to the driveway. Tears were streaming down the girl's face. Amy forced herself to look away from the mirrors, but her heart was dying, and she could hear Ruby's wails as she drove away.

Lord, have mercy on us all.

"Make her stay! Daddy, make her stay!" Ruby raced toward Amy's car, and Nash had to grab her to stop her. She thrashed about, desperately trying to free herself, constantly shouting, "Make her stay!"

He wrapped his arms around her, holding her tightly until she stopped trying to break free. Tears streamed down her face, and her huge, gulping sobs killed something inside him. Finally, she stilled, whispering, "Don't let Miss Amy leave. Tell her I'll be good."

Nash couldn't stop the pressure building in his chest. He'd pushed Amy out of his life as easily as he'd walked away a decade ago. And this time he hadn't only ruined his life. He'd ruined Ruby's, as well.

And he had no idea why.

He carried Ruby into the house.

"Why'd you tell her to leave? She didn't want to. She said so. And you told her to go. Why, Daddy? Why?"

Why, indeed?

"I don't know. I've got to think about it. Let's give Amy time to cool off." He set Ruby on the couch. She covered her face with her tiny hands and ran upstairs, bawling. The sound of her door slamming rattled his entire body.

Smoke billowed from the patio, and he jogged outside. The steaks were black and smelled awful. He flicked the gas off and refrained from kicking the grill.

Charred meat. A brokenhearted little girl. And the best woman he'd ever met had just driven away.

It was all his fault. Every drop of it.

He tossed the black steaks onto a plate to cool off.

Amy's words about Hank and his mother kept running through his brain. He wouldn't argue that his mother had been supremely unqualified to have kids. But Hank hadn't used Nash. And Nash would never put Amy in the same category as either of them, anyway.

What did she know?

If she knew how bad his childhood had been, she'd have driven off long ago.

But she did know. Maybe he hadn't told her every rotten story, all the twisted details, but she knew. And she hadn't left him.

She hadn't treated him differently. She hadn't judged him or looked down on him, and she certainly hadn't walked away from him.

She'd been his rock. The person he least deserved to have on his side.

Ten years ago, he'd blamed his mother for the way he had left Amy. But maybe it had been a convenient lie—the same lie he was trying to sell himself now—that he was doing it for her own good.

Could she be right? Maybe he didn't trust her.

Did he trust anybody? Or was he so messed up that he chased every good thing away? Everyone acted like he was some sort of superstar for riding ornery bulls, but he hadn't been brave.

Every thud of being launched onto the ground, each time his arm was yanked out of its socket, every bruise, kick, broken bone—all had given him a sense of relief from the yawning hole inside him.

And each time he'd cheated death, he'd known he didn't deserve another chance.

Yet, somehow he was still here.

He sat at the table, dropping his head in his hands.

God, I thought I was doing all right. I made the most of my life the only way I knew how, the only way it made sense. But I'm more empty and confused than ever. What's the point? Why am I here? Why did You make me?

He thought of his time at the group foster home. All the church services with Big Bob and Dottie. The many times Dottie had told him, "Jesus loves you. Nothing— not one thing—can separate you from His love. Got that, hotshot?"

Dottie and her "hotshot." Maybe a talk with lil' mama would get his thoughts straight. He swiped his phone and called.

Chapter Fourteen

Amy unlocked the door to her store and flipped on the lights to the back room. Her fury had cooled, replaced by desolation. She hadn't allowed herself to cry yet, and on the drive home, she'd concentrated on all the ways Nash had failed her in the past. She should never have let him back into her life. The blame was all hers.

And she was tired of taking the blame.

She'd been convinced something was wrong with her to make Nash leave. Then she'd grown certain of it when John left, too. But the only thing wrong with her was her choice in men. They were the problem. Always had been.

But it meant she was part of the problem, too, because she kept falling for the wrong guys.

God, why didn't You equip me with the radar other women have? I need some sort of internal alert system that would say, "Hey, he's a keeper. He won't let you down," or, "Nope, don't even think about that guy. He's as unreliable as they come." Why? Why, God?

Ruby's cries kept echoing in her head. She'd broken her promise to Ruby. She'd told the little girl she was only there for her. But Amy hadn't turned around when Ruby had run out crying. The child must have witnessed their argument.

Amy's lungs kept squeezing and tightening, and it was so hard to breathe. How had everything gone wrong in such a short amount of time? Just a couple of hours ago she'd gotten the call from Lexi's friend, never realizing it would cause her life to implode.

She trudged to the showroom. The store had always brought her peace and joy. Gleaming hardwood floors, rugs, the fabrics folded and displayed just so, the quilts hanging on the walls. Her quilts. Her gaze climbed the wall to the first quilt she'd ever made. It wasn't for sale.

Memories crashed back of stitching it by hand the year after Nash left. At the time, she'd been piecing together scraps of material in all different colors and shapes. She hadn't known there was a name for it—a crazy quilt. And she never would have guessed the final product would be a thing of beauty. It had been a way out of the pain at the time.

The jewel-tone fabrics had been scraps in one of her mother's bins of craft materials for projects at the senior center. The purple, midnight blue and wine red fabrics below the center of the quilt still held her tears. She'd stitched the section after Christmas that year. Each added piece had allowed her to truly let go of her hopes that Nash would realize he'd made a terrible mistake and come back.

The colors blended together in rich imperfection, a melding of each dream she'd been forced to let go.

She took out a step stool and set it under the hanging quilt. Three steps up, and she pressed the bottom of the quilt to her cheek. The instant the material touched her skin Nash's face in her rearview mirror came back to her.

No, I don't want to remember! I want to forget!

He wasn't the man for her. He couldn't love her the way she needed, and she was done giving her love to people who couldn't reciprocate it.

She stepped down from the ladder. The crazy quilt had been scrapped together with her discarded love. Because Nash hadn't wanted what she'd desperately wanted to give him.

And he still refused to accept what she wanted to give…

She clasped her hands. She'd been trying to deny she loved him. But she'd loved him all along.

She'd always loved him.

And she couldn't keep giving her heart to someone who didn't want it.

She was worth more than that.

After locking up the store, she slowly made her way to the apartment. The quilt she'd been making for Ruby sat in blocks on the worktable. Her cell phone dinged. She swiped, hoping it was Nash, but it was a reminder from Mom to stop by tomorrow. Her fumbling fingers accidentally pressed her photos.

The first picture greeting her was Ruby on Nash's lap here in the apartment.

The phone dropped from her hands, and she covered her face, crying desperate tears.

It was really over. Her fantasy of life with Nash and Ruby—of being their family—had come to an end.

She did the only thing she could when faced with a gaping hole in her heart. She picked up the quilt she was making for Ruby and began to hand-stitch the blocks together. Tears dropped onto the fabric, one after the other.

She'd gotten over Nash once. She'd do it again.

* * *

"It's not like you to call me, hotshot. What's wrong?"

Normally he'd respond with "Nothing's wrong," but he was way past denial. "I need some straight-up, godly advice, lil' mama."

Silence greeted him. "This *is* Nash, correct?"

"Yes, Dottie, it's me." He fought exasperation. "Are you going to help or not?"

"Well, don't get your britches in a bunch. I'm not used to any of you boys asking for advice."

"Sorry." And he was. It wasn't her fault he'd screwed up his life. He never should have left Amy all those years ago. Amy was right—he'd taken the easy way out and used his mother as an excuse to avoid trusting in a future with her.

"Is this about buttercup?"

"No, it's about puddin'." He couldn't believe he'd actually referred to Amy as puddin'.

"Ah, I'm glad. Looks like you kids have patched up your problems. I always thought you were perfect for each other."

"Well, I ripped a big old hole back into those problems. But I don't know why."

"You'd better explain it to me, hon. I'm not a mind reader."

Explain it? He didn't even know where to begin. He sighed. "It all started the day I met with Pastor Moore. I can't even tell you my shock when Amy walked in to be Ruby's mentor."

"I'm guessing her shock was equal to yours."

"More, probably…" He told Dottie everything. How selfless Amy had been in helping Ruby, how he admired Amy's talent and career, how they'd become friends again and how he had deeper feelings, way deeper than he had thought possible. Finally, he admitted how he'd pushed her away.

"Well, you know lettin' a cat out of the bag is a lot easier than puttin' it back in," Dottie said.

"I guess." He scrunched his nose, trying to decipher what she meant. "Actually, I don't know why that applies to this situation."

"I don't know why you just up and left her all those years ago, hon. If you can figure that out, you'll have a good chance at figuring out why you're pushing her away now. I'm pretty sure the reason is one and the same."

"Why do you think I did it?" He held his breath, hoping for the answer, the one that would make sense.

"Oh, Nash, I could give you a hundred reasons, but if none of them are the right one, they won't matter. You need to get your Bible out and pray."

Disappointment hit him hard. Dottie was making him figure things out for himself? He wanted her to give him the answers.

"Get your Bible out. Right now. And start praying. And if you get an answer to those prayers, don't be afraid to call me anytime to watch buttercup if you need to go over and talk to puddin'. Even if it's the middle of the night. I'll understand."

"Okay, Dottie. Thank you."

"I love you, hon."

"Love you, too."

After hanging up, he did as he was told. He went upstairs to his bedroom, grabbed his Bible and headed back down to the kitchen table. He sat and paused. *Father, I don't know what my problem is, but I'm asking for Your help figuring it out. I've got Ruby to think about now. I can't go messing everyone's lives up. I need You.*

He took a moment to let his thoughts clear. Then he opened the Bible and flipped through to his favorite psalm—thirty-seven. Trailing his finger, he found the beginning of the seventh verse: "Rest in the LORD, and wait patiently for him."

He'd found the verse last year. He'd struggled with being still—with resting—his entire life. Patience didn't come naturally to him. But taking matters into his own hands? He got that. Oh, how he got it.

When he was young, he'd wanted a mother who loved him, but he got one who abused him. Then he'd wanted a father, and Hank had showed up, but in many ways, Amy was right. Hank had abused him, too.

The night Hank died stood in his mind as fresh as if it had happened last week. The summer heat had been scorching all weekend. Dusk had fallen. The lights beamed onto the arena floor. Nash had placed second in the junior bull ride—his bull calf had been rambunctious—and he was hanging out by the chutes, joking with the other guys who'd competed. The announcer called Hank's name, and Nash had been taken aback. Weren't the barrel races going on? Hank rarely competed in those. He'd tried to peer over the chutes, but he'd had to run around them to see what was happening. The gasp from the crowd slowed his steps, and when he'd finally been able to see, Hank was on the ground, the horse scrambling to roll off him. Hank wasn't moving. He'd died instantly.

In that moment, seeing Hank's lifeless body, Nash's world collapsed. Without Hank and summers and the rodeo, all Nash had left was a drug-addicted mother. A life full of chaos.

His chest now burned with pent-up sobs. *I needed you, Hank. I loved you. You were the only man I looked up to when I was young. I wanted to be just like you. Why'd you have to die?*

He'd put the night out of his mind for almost twenty years. Refused to remember in case it broke him.

Would it break him tonight?

Did you know I did it, Hank? I became a world champion bull rider. Remember how we used to drive those lonely highways, talking about what we'd do when we hit it big? Well, I actually made it. And I never would have if it wasn't for you. I wish you'd have been there. You would have loved it. You would have chewed me out every time I came in second and told me exactly what I had done wrong. I'd have listened, too, because I trusted you. I think you were the last person I trusted with the most important parts of me. When you died, part of me died with you.

He gave in to the emotions. Cried until there was nothing left. He'd never grieved Hank, and it felt good and right to feel the pain of losing him. Finally, he lifted his head and stared at the refrigerator.

Drawings, coloring pages, cut-outs and more filled the fridge door. Ruby's handiwork. All because of Amy.

Amy.

The only person who had never—not once—given him a reason to doubt her intentions. She'd loved him unconditionally a decade ago. And now?

The woman he'd treated so shabbily was more honorable than anyone he'd ever met. She could have been spiteful and full of revenge. Could have spit in his face when she learned about Ruby and the lies he'd told her about not having a mother. But she hadn't. Instead, she'd gone so far above anything he'd ever known to set aside her own feelings in order to help Ruby.

He loved her. He didn't deserve her, but his heart was filled to the brim with love for that woman.

A picture of three stick figures holding hands under a sun caught his eye. The scene told him everything he needed to know.

Amy was Ruby's Hank.

And for him, Amy was more. She was the difference between a glass of pure water and one of thick mud. A dreary overcast day and a spectacular sunny day. He couldn't do life without her, and he refused to pretend he could.

He didn't know how to win her back. But he had to try.

"Tell me exactly what he said, and don't leave out a word." Lexi crossed one leg over the other at six thirty Saturday morning.

Amy felt bad for waking Lexi so early but was relieved that she'd insisted on coming over. They both held matching pink floral teacups and saucers.

"I told him about the job offer, and I honestly think he tuned out most of what I said." Amy perched on the edge of the chair next to the couch. Her tea lay untouched in her hands.

"Why do you think that?"

"Because he told me to take the job." Amy hadn't slept much last night, and the bags under her eyes felt heavier than bolts of upholstery fabric. "He thinks I'll regret not taking it."

"But you don't want the job." Concern hooded Lexi's eyes. "I'm sorry, Amy. I never thought she'd offer you a position and expect you to move. I thought she'd love your fabrics and want to collaborate on pillows or something."

"Don't be sorry. No matter how many times I told him I didn't want the job and wasn't taking it, he kept pushing me to leave. I think he was looking for an excuse to put the brakes on our relationship."

Lexi raised her eyebrows and took a sip of tea. "I know all about that. Clint and I got into a huge fight before he proposed. I didn't see him for a few days. Thought he'd left for good."

"Yes, but he came back. I don't think this will have a happy ending."

"You don't know that, Amy. Remember, darkness comes before morning. Anyway, tell me the rest."

"And sometimes darkness just gets darker." Amy set her teacup on the coffee table. "I got tired of arguing with him about this dumb job offer. Then it hit me. Maybe his messed up childhood is to blame. Maybe he's not capable of loving me the way I expect."

Lexi nodded. "Clint's childhood was pretty bad, too. But he got the courage to give love a chance."

"Well, I don't see it happening in our case. I yelled at him and ran to my car. And Ruby must have heard because she came flying out the front door as I was driving away. I can still hear her wailing." Amy slumped in the chair. "I can't get her cries or Nash's face out of my mind."

Lexi cringed. "Did he look pretty mad?"

"No…he looked…" She didn't want to think about it, but his face was there. Pale, shocked, blue around the lips. She gasped, bringing her fingers to her mouth. "Oh, no."

"What?"

Amy crossed the room to the window. Why hadn't

she realized this earlier? Nash had looked exactly the same as Ruby had on the first day he'd dropped her off at Amy's apartment.

Terrified. Shattered.

She tried to undo the knot of truths twisting around each other in her mind. Ruby had been severely neglected. And when Amy had asked how Nash knew what Ruby had been through, he'd told her he knew from experience.

His experience.

Ruby and Nash were one and the same.

Same mother. Same horrible childhood. Same desperate need for an anchor they could trust.

Except Ruby had gotten out of that nightmare of a life when she was still young, and the only anchor Nash had found was Hank until he died. But maybe Amy had been his anchor, too. Then his mom had intervened.

No wonder he had such a hard time with trust.

And his face last night…he *did* trust her. If she had to guess, she'd say he trusted her more than anyone else in the world. But look at how Ruby had feared Nash would leave her. It had taken time and patience for Ruby to finally believe he'd always stay.

Maybe Nash needed time and patience to trust Amy wouldn't disappear the way other people in his life had.

"What is it, Amy?" Lexi twisted in her seat.

She returned and sank into the chair. "I just realized something. I don't think I've ever truly understood why Nash is the way he is."

"Is that a good thing or a bad thing?"

"I'm not sure." She bit her lower lip. "You know how I told you Ruby was terrified of staying alone with me when I first met her?"

"Yes, the poor little thing. It broke my heart when you told me she'd worried Nash didn't want her anymore and she thought he'd just left her with you. What must have happened to her to make her think something like that."

"I know. It was so heartbreaking. And this is going to sound weird, but I think, deep down, Nash has the same fear when it comes to me."

Lexi took a sip of tea before answering. "How do you mean? He's worried you'll dump him?"

"No, not that. I think he wants to believe I won't hurt him, but given his past, he can't quite bring himself to trust it. Does that make sense?"

"Yes. Absolutely. I think you nailed it."

Amy selected a shortbread cookie from the plate on the coffee table. Lexi munched on one, too.

"What are you going to do now?" Lexi asked, brushing crumbs from her hands.

"I don't know."

"You love him, don't you?"

Amy nodded, tears threatening once more.

"But do you think he can ever emotionally give you what you need?"

Amy sighed. Ruby had blossomed with Nash's patience and constant assurances he'd never leave her. But Ruby was four. Nash was over thirty and had experienced more hardships.

"I know you want to get married and have a family, Amy. What if he never gets to the point where he can commit to you, heart and soul?"

Why did Lexi ask the toughest questions? Amy's chest felt so raw. If Nash couldn't commit heart and soul...

"If that's the case, there will never be anything between us, and I'll have to convince him to allow me to continue my relationship with Ruby."

"It will be hard."

"My life usually is hard."

"I can't argue with that." Lexi clasped her hands together. "Does he know how you feel about him?"

"I haven't said the *l* word if that's what you're asking."

"Don't you think you should before you make any decisions?"

This conversation was giving her indigestion. She'd already been brave and asked him about marriage and kids. Now she had to tell him she loved him? After he'd let her leave?

Hadn't he been the one to walk away last time? Not to mention she'd set aside her feelings to help him with Ruby. He should be the one begging her to stay, telling her he loved her, being vulnerable for once in his life.

Amy, you know the fruit of the Spirit is love, joy, kindness, gentleness and all that.

She'd been kind. She'd been gentle. He could do the love and joy part.

Didn't you ask the good Lord to send you out to the harvest? Did you only do it for a reward?

Shame sunk like a pit in her gut. Nash didn't owe her anything. She'd entered their arrangement with one intention—to spend time with a little girl. It wasn't his fault she'd fallen right back in love with him.

God, remind me You're enough. You've always been enough for me.

"If you don't tell him, you might always wonder, 'What if…'" Lexi said. "I'd hate to see you with regrets. I know how much you care about him and Ruby."

"I do care about them. More than I ever thought possible. Nash listens to me, is interested in my life, and he cares. I know he cares. I just don't know if he cares enough. As for Ruby—she's like a piece of my heart. I think I'd give just about anything to raise her as my own child."

"You have to tell him."

Amy nodded.

"Now. Go." Lexi stood, pointing to the door. "Before you have second thoughts."

"I look terrible, Lexi." She couldn't go over there with her hair an unruly squirrel's nest and her face a splotchy mess.

"Well, get in the shower and slap some makeup on. But you have to go to his house this morning and tell him the truth—tell him you love him and you'll never let him down."

Amy gasped. How had Lexi known the exact words they'd thrown at each other? Was that what Nash had really meant when he'd told her he'd only let her down? Had he been conveying his fears *she* would let *him* down?

"Promise me you're going over there. Tell him." Lexi wagged her finger at Amy.

"I promise."

"You mean it?"

"Yes. You're right. I don't want to live with regrets. It's better to be open and honest with him and lay it all out. Then I'll know where I stand, and I'll be able to move forward."

Lexi hugged her. "Call me when it's over."

"I will." Amy walked her to the door. "Thanks."

After Lexi left, Amy headed straight for the shower. She might as well follow Lexi's advice and get this over with. She just hoped she'd be the winner in love for once.

Chapter Fifteen

A tap on Nash's shoulder woke him. He lifted his head from where it rested on his arm, groaning at the crick in his neck. He'd fallen asleep at the kitchen table. Wiping his mouth, he squinted at the clock. Seven in the morning.

"Daddy?"

"What?" He shot to a sitting position. "What is it, RuRu?"

She stood before him with dark circles under her eyes and the expression of a basset hound. Her long blond hair rippled down her back. She wore a pink princess nightgown, and bare toes snuck out beneath the hem. She held a shoebox in her hands.

"Will you take me over to Miss Amy's? I have all my best things. I'll give her all of it if she'll stay."

Rip my heart open first thing why don't you, Ruby?

"Honey, that's not how it works." He lifted her, settling her on his lap. "Miss Amy spends time with you because she wants to. She adores you. It makes her happy to frost cupcakes and color and all the things she does with you."

"But she likes spending time with you, too, Daddy. Her eyes crinkle up—they look like they're smiling—

when you talk to her, and she's always as nice as can be to you."

He shifted his jaw. Ruby was right. But what could he say? *Hey, kid, I know Miss Amy is all that and a bag of chips, but I blew it. More than once. And she deserves better than me.*

"I prayed last night to Jesus just like you told me to." Tears began forming in her eyes. He swiped them away with his thumb.

"I did, too, RuRu."

"Did He forgive you?"

"Yes. He always forgives us when we repent." Man, this kid was hitting home the truths this morning.

"If you say you're sorry to Miss Amy, she'll forgive you, too." Ruby caressed his cheek with her itty-bitty hand.

"It's more complicated than that."

"Why?"

Why? I don't know. Nothing makes sense anymore.

"I hurt Miss Amy a long time ago. I was her boyfriend, and I left her."

"Mama left me cuz I was a bad girl. Miss Amy said I wasn't, but…" Ruby couldn't sound more distraught. "Miss Amy's never been bad. Why'd you leave her?"

"You had nothing to do with your mother leaving. Nothing. You weren't a bad girl." His heart felt like a shredded, pulverized piece of meat. "Your mother used drugs and never should have left you. You deserved more. Still deserve more. But you need to understand something else, Ruby. Nobody is perfect. Not even Miss Amy. And it's okay to not be perfect. God loves us and He sent His Son to die for us to take away our sins. So even if you did something really naughty, God forgives you and still loves you. Does that make sense?"

"Miss Amy told me that, too." She gave him a pitiful nod. "I want her to stay. She'll forgive you."

How could he explain to Ruby he was afraid he'd hurt Amy again? He didn't know how, but what if…

"Daddy, I don't want her to go to Denver. Can't we go to her 'partment and tell her not to go? I'll give her Brownie and Fluffy and Chantilly."

His gaze fell to the box Ruby had set on the table. He could see all of the contents. An apple. A baggie full of fish-shaped crackers. All of the paper hearts they'd cut out together. A placemat with a brown horse and red cloud scribbled on it. A box of crayons. Every eraser and sticker she'd gotten from the Easter egg hunt. The ribbon he'd tied around Fluffy.

Those simple treasures were everything to Ruby, and she was willing to give them all to Amy if she'd just stay.

Shame hit him. It was more than he'd offered Amy.

Lord, I'm sorry. This little girl has opened my eyes to the meaning of sacrifice. If You'll show me the way, I want to do the same. Amy gave me everything good. I want to give her that, too. And as much as I tell myself I'm not worthy of her and I've done too much to hurt her—I can't believe it anymore. I've got to accept Your forgiveness. I want to embrace Your love.

"Please, Daddy? Please?"

"You don't have to give Amy anything, Ruby." He took a deep breath, terrified and exhilarated at what he was about to say. "I love Miss Amy. I think she might love me, too. And here's what I'm going to do. I'm going to take a shower and drop you off to have breakfast with Dottie. Then I'm driving over to Miss Amy's and I'm going to tell her how much I love her and beg her to forgive me. How does that sound?"

Ruby's eyes grew wide with hope and excitement. "You mean Miss Amy might be your girlfriend?"

He hoped more than a girlfriend. The engagement ring he'd purchased a decade ago still sat in his drawer. He'd love nothing more than to see it on Amy's finger. Hadn't they wasted enough time?

He gave her a big smile. "I sure hope so, RuRu. Now you get dressed while I shower, okay?"

"Okay! Hurry!"

She was an old dishrag; the mirror proved it. Amy applied another layer of concealer under her eyes. Still puffy and dark. Telling Nash she loved him would be much easier if she looked her best. An impossible task at the moment. Swiping a burgundy lipstick over her lips, she puckered them and stood back.

Yikes.

Maybe she should get a good night's sleep and do this tomorrow.

No, she'd promised Lexi she would tell him today.

Ugh. Consciences. Who needed them?

She drew her shoulders back. *Lord, I know You made me strong enough to do this, but sometimes I get tired of being strong. Will You be my strength?*

Someone knocked on the door. "Amy, are you in there?"

Nash! Her pulse sprinted as she straightened her shirt, trying not to panic. She went to the door.

"What are you doing here?" She drank him in, from his cowboy hat to his plaid button-down, belt buckle, jeans and cowboy boots. His face was scruffy, like he'd forgotten to shave.

He stepped inside and closed the door behind him. Gently took her by the biceps. His jaw shifted.

"I love you." He stared into her eyes, and she spiraled into their intensity. Trying to get her head on straight, she blinked. More than once.

"I love you," he said again. "And I am not going to walk away this time. You were right. I didn't trust you but only because I never fully trusted myself. For the record, I *was* afraid my mother would hurt you—I grew up with abuse, and not just from her but from the men around us—but it went deeper. Part of it was Hank. Not the way you think, though."

She wanted to say something, but she held back. Instead, she savored his calloused hands on her skin, his light grip on her arms.

"When I lost Hank, I lost the one good thing in my life. And I think part of me believed I could never trust in anything good lasting forever."

Amy bit her lip. What he said made sense.

"So I left you. And I spent years taking risks, punishing my body, seeing how far I could go to escape the fact I wasn't with you. And then when I returned, you were so spectacular. I mean, I had a child in tow. And I'd never met anyone as generous and selfless and forgiving as you. You are too good for me. But I never stopped loving you, Amy, and this love—what's in my heart—is so much more than I can put in words. I don't expect you to believe me, but I would do anything for you. Please, tell me you forgive me. For leaving you back then. For pushing you away last night."

She inhaled deeply, shaking her head in wonder. "I love you, too, Nash."

"You really love me?" His body was close to hers.

"Yes." She nodded, unable to tear her eyes from his. "But I need you to hear me out about something."

His face fell, but he nodded. "Okay. Your turn."

*   *   *

Nash braced himself. He had a feeling he was about to hear something that would shatter his dreams.

"I realized something."

Here it comes. Take it like a man.

"You're Ruby."

He twisted his lips, frowning. "What?"

She nodded, her pretty brown eyes sincere. "You and Ruby—you're the same. Same eyes. Same forehead. Same mother. Same awful start to life. You both had terrible childhoods. Neither of you could trust the one person you should've been able to trust with your entire heart. And the look on Ruby's face the first time you tried to leave her here—the terrified, shattered expression? You had the same one last night, Nash. I'm not telling you this to make you feel bad. I want you to understand that, whether you know it or not, you share some of the fears Ruby's overcoming. The main difference between you and her is she got out when she was young. You've never had anyone you could truly trust."

He took off his hat, running his fingers through his hair. Amy was right. He'd put some of it together last night, but he'd never realized the issues Ruby was dealing with were issues he needed to deal with, as well.

"And, Nash." Amy took his hand in hers. "You can trust me. I know it's hard for you, so I'll be patient. I love you, and I'll never let you down. I'll never abandon you or use you."

This woman. His breath caught in his throat as he stared up at the ceiling. She slayed him. Just when he thought she couldn't get any better…

"Amy, I know I can trust you. With all my heart. With my soul." He reached into his jeans pocket and took out the box. Clumsily, he dropped to one knee, trying not to wince on the way down. *Please, God, let me not ruin this. Let her say yes.*

"Ten years ago, I bought the house and land I'm living on as a gift for you. I didn't tell you about it because I'd also purchased something else, and I wanted both to be a surprise." He opened the box and took out the ring. "Even though the surprise is a decade late, there is nothing in the world I want more than to be your husband. You've showered me with goodness, and I want to shower you with whatever your heart desires for the rest of your life. Will you marry me?"

Her jaw dropped and she cupped her hands over her mouth, her eyes filling with tears.

"Oh, Nash!" She pulled him up to stand. "Yes! I'll marry you."

"Don't you even want to see the ring?" He held it out to her.

Through her tears, she beamed, laughing. "Yes."

He slid the ring on her finger. From the way her eyes widened, he guessed she liked it.

"Wow." She held her arm out, hand up, admiring the large diamond. "That's some rock."

"And you're some woman." He tugged her closer and lowered his lips to hers. Perfection. Sliding his arms around her waist, he drank in her sweetness, dazzled at the thought he'd be kissing her every day for the rest of his life.

Finally, he broke free. They grinned at each other. No words were needed.

"So you know this means you're going to be a mommy."

Her smile arched like a brilliant rainbow. "I want to be Ruby's mommy."

"And how do you feel about adding more little cowboys and cowgirls as soon as possible?"

"As soon as possible. Nash, you have no idea how much I've longed for children. But if for whatever reason it doesn't happen, Ruby will be more than enough."

"I love you." He kissed her again. "You're really mine?"

"Forever." She wound her arms around his neck.

"Let's go tell Ruby."

Feeling lighter than a helium balloon, Amy held Nash's hand as they walked to Dottie's Diner to tell Ruby the big news. What if Ruby didn't want them to get married? Well, there was no sense in borrowing trouble. They'd find out soon enough.

Lord, You answered my prayers in the most spectacular fashion. Thank You! Please let Ruby be happy with our news. I don't want to bring turmoil to her life. I love her so much.

"After you, my lady." He held the diner's door open, and she sailed through under his arm.

"Miss Amy!" Ruby hopped off her stool and flew into her arms. Amy smoothed her hair and held her close. Ruby smiled up at her. "You didn't leave!"

"Is that what you thought?" Amy knelt. "I would never go somewhere without telling you goodbye. But, Ruby, I don't have any plans to leave. I love Sweet Dreams. My life is here."

Ruby hugged her as if her life depended on it.

"Come on, let's get out of the way." Nash directed them to an empty booth. Once they settled, he rested his elbows on the table. "Miss Amy and I have something to tell you. We know it might bring up some emotions in you, so don't be afraid to tell us the truth about how you feel, okay?"

Worry wrinkled her little forehead, but she nodded.

"I asked Miss Amy to marry me, and she said yes."

Ruby's face transformed from scared to awestruck. "You mean Miss Amy will be my mommy?"

"Yes, RuRu, that's exactly what it means." Nash looked serious.

Amy turned to Ruby. "I know this is sudden, honey, so if you're—"

Ruby wrapped her arms around Amy's neck and began to cry. Amy patted her back, murmuring comfort. Was the girl happy or sad? Then Ruby lifted her head.

"I pray to Jesus every night that you'll be my mommy, Miss Amy. And He answered! You were right! He does answer prayers."

Amy was unprepared for the emotions swelling within her. This girl's love—it amazed her. *Lord, I forgot You're listening to more than my prayers. Thank You for answering both our prayers.*

"I love you very much, Ruby, and I can't wait to be your mommy." She kissed Ruby's cheek, and Ruby climbed onto her lap. "You're the daughter I've always dreamed about."

Amy met Nash's eyes, and from the looks of it, he was having a hard time with his emotions, too. She reached across the table. He took her hand. And they smiled at each other.

God had saved His best for them all.

Epilogue

Today was no ordinary day, not for Amy Deerson, at least. Scratch that—Amy *Bolton*. She'd just married the man of her dreams and had become the mother of her favorite little girl in the whole world. Pausing in the church's entryway, she took advantage of the rare moment alone. *Thank You, God!*

The doors opened, and a September wind gusted, kicking up the back of her veil. Nash grinned, taking one step toward her and sweeping her into his arms. He easily carried her down the steps and to the waiting limo. Ruby had gone on ahead with Dottie and Big Bob.

"It's a good thing I've been working out with Shane, or I might have missed out on carrying my beautiful bride." He slid into the back seat of the limo next to her, shutting the door. Then he drew her close. "Finally. I've waited all day to be alone with you, Amy."

"That's Mrs. Bolton to you, hotshot." She barely noticed the countryside as they drove the short distance into town.

"Puddin', I don't care what you want me to call you as long as you're mine."

"Oh, I'm yours. You can't get rid of me." She couldn't believe how much her life had changed in the few short months they'd been engaged. She'd received the strike offs of her fabric line, and the final products would be finished in time for next May's International Quilt Market trade show. In the meantime, she'd started another portfolio to sell. Construction on Nash's training center was coming along nicely, and he would be opening it in the spring. She, her mom and Lexi had spent last weekend packing up Amy's personal items and moving them to Nash's house. Her house, now. She'd decided to turn the entire apartment into a quilting studio. She might even give sewing workshops there in the future.

"I feel like I'm forgetting something." Nash had a goofy grin on his face.

"What could you possibly be forgetting?"

"What it was like to not have you in my life." He kissed her. "Now I don't have to spend a single day without you."

"Oh, Nash…"

The limo stopped in front of the Department Store, Lexi's reception hall. Naturally, they'd hired her to plan the wedding, and she'd pulled off a spectacular event in a short amount of time.

"Does this mean I have to share you again?" Nash pulled a face.

"Yep." She gave him a quick kiss. "When we get inside, I'm going to find Ruby. I have something for her."

"You do?" He helped her out of the limo and tucked her arm under his. "What is it?"

"You can join us if you're curious."

"I am curious. But I admit I'll take any excuse to be with you."

They entered the building and applause erupted. Wade and Clint, clad in tuxedoes, rushed up, clapping Nash on the back and congratulating Amy. Only Marshall couldn't make it. His twin sister had gone into labor with quadruplets. Four babies? Amy didn't blame him for missing the wedding. She searched for Ruby, excitement growing when she spotted her. "There she is."

"I'll come with you." Nash's gaze burned with love. He excused himself and took her by the hand. The three of them climbed the grand staircase to the room Lexi had prepared for Amy.

"How did you like being the flower girl?" Amy knelt next to Ruby. The girl wore a white dress and a tiara like Amy's.

"I loved it! I sprinkled the flowers all over the aisle just like you showed me."

"You did a great job." Amy straightened, reaching for the box she'd brought over last night. "Now that it's official, I wanted to give you this."

Ruby held the large wrapped box in her hand. "What is it?" She sounded breathless.

"Open it." Amy smiled, hoping she would love it.

Ruby tore off the paper and lifted the lid. Bringing her hands to her mouth, she said, "Oh."

"Go ahead. Pick it up." Amy nodded to her.

Ruby held up the pink and purple quilt with the kitten pattern.

"I made it for you."

"It's the colors I loved, and it's got kitties!" Ruby drew it to her chin, rocking back and forth with a huge smile on her face. "I love it!"

She'd poured her love into the quilt, and it made her happy that Ruby appreciated it.

Nash put his arm around Amy. "Wow, I can't believe you made this." He crouched before Ruby. "What do you say?"

"Thank you, Mommy!"

Amy gasped in wonder. She really was a mommy now.

"You've given me the best gift in the world, Ruby." Amy kissed her forehead then hugged her. "And, Nash, you've given me the best gift in the world, too."

Nash drew the two of them into his arms. "You've got it backward. You're the gift, Amy. I will never let you go."

"Never, ever?"

"Never, ever. That's a promise I'll gladly keep."

* * * * *

If you enjoyed this story, pick up the first book in Jill Kemerer's Wyoming Cowboys miniseries:

THE RANCHER'S MISTLETOE BRIDE

And don't miss these other books by Jill Kemerer:

UNEXPECTED FAMILY
HOMETOWN HERO'S REDEMPTION

Available now from Love Inspired!

Find more great reads at www.LoveInspired.com

Dear Reader,

Do you ever feel torn between gratitude for the blessings in your life and envy of others who have things you still want? I struggle with this. I can wake up in the morning, praising God for my family, my health and the opportunity to write for a living. Two hours later I'm jealous and grumbling at a Facebook post someone shared. Like Amy at the Easter egg hunt, though, I keep turning back to focus on God's providence. I try my best to keep a "Send me" spirit to do His will. I fail sometimes, but thankfully, we don't have to be perfect!

My prayer is for you to walk daily with the Lord and to embrace obedience even when it feels impossible. He loves to bless His children. You never know—He might bless you beyond your wildest dreams!

I love to hear from readers, so please email me at jill@jillkemerer.com or write to PO Box 2802, Whitehouse, Ohio 43571. Bless you!

Jill Kemerer

COMING NEXT MONTH FROM
Love Inspired®

Available June 19, 2018

HIS NEW AMISH FAMILY
The Amish Bachelors • by Patricia Davids

Desperate to stop her *Englisch* cousin from selling the farm her uncle promised to her, widow Clara Fisher seeks the help of auctioneer Paul Bowman. Paul's always been a wandering spirit, but will sweet, stubborn Clara and her children suddenly fill his empty life with family and love?

HER FORGIVING AMISH HEART
Women of Lancaster County • by Rebecca Kertz

Leah Stoltzfus hasn't forgiven Henry Yoder for betraying her family years earlier. But Henry is a changed man. And when a family secret is unearthed, shaking Leah to her core, he's determined to support her. If only she could leave the past behind and open her heart to him...

THE SOLDIER'S REDEMPTION
Redemption Ranch • by Lee Tobin McClain

Finn Gallagher's drawn to his new rescue-dog caretaker, Kayla White, and her little boy. But the single mother's running from something in her past. And as he begins wishing the little family could be *his*, Finn must convince her to trust him with her secret.

FALLING FOR THE COWGIRL
Big Heart Ranch • by Tina Radcliffe

Hiring Amanda "AJ" McAlester as his assistant at the Big Heart Ranch isn't foreman Travis Maxwell's first choice—but his sisters insist she's perfect for the job. But with money on the line, AJ and her innovative ideas could put him at risk of losing everything...including his heart.

HIS TWO LITTLE BLESSINGS
Liberty Creek • by Mia Ross

When the school board threatens to cut her art program, Emma Calhoun plans to fight for the job she loves. And with banker Rick Marshall on board to help, she might just succeed. But will the handsome widower and his sweet little girls burrow their way into her heart?

THE COWBOY'S LITTLE GIRL
Bent Creek Blessings • by Kat Brookes

Cowboy Tucker Wade discovers he has a daughter he never knew about when his late wife's twin sister shows up on his doorstep. Now it's up to Autumn Myers to decide if he can be the kind of daddy her niece deserves.

LICNM0618

Get 4 FREE REWARDS!

We'll send you 2 FREE Books plus 2 FREE Mystery Gifts.

Love Inspired® books feature contemporary inspirational romances with Christian characters facing the challenges of life and love.

FREE
Value Over
$20

YES! Please send me 2 FREE Love Inspired® Romance novels and my 2 FREE mystery gifts (gifts are worth about $10 retail). After receiving them, if I don't wish to receive any more books, I can return the shipping statement marked "cancel." If I don't cancel, I will receive 6 brand-new novels every month and be billed just $5.24 for the regular-print edition or $5.74 each for the larger-print edition in the U.S., or $5.74 each for the regular-print edition or $6.24 each for the larger-print edition in Canada. That's a savings of at least 13% off the cover price. It's quite a bargain! Shipping and handling is just 50¢ per book in the U.S. and 75¢ per book in Canada*. I understand that accepting the 2 free books and gifts places me under no obligation to buy anything. I can always return a shipment and cancel at any time. The free books and gifts are mine to keep no matter what I decide.

Choose one: ☐ Love Inspired® Romance
 Regular-Print
 (105/305 IDN GMY4)

☐ Love Inspired® Romance
 Larger-Print
 (122/322 IDN GMY4)

Name (please print)

Address   Apt. #

City   State/Province   Zip/Postal Code

Mail to the **Reader Service:**
IN U.S.A.: P.O. Box 1341, Buffalo, NY 14240-8531
IN CANADA: P.O. Box 603, Fort Erie, Ontario L2A 5X3

Want to try two free books from another series? Call 1-800-873-8635 or visit www.ReaderService.com.

Her family's future in the balance, can Clara Fisher find a way to save her home?

Read on for a sneak preview of
HIS NEW AMISH FAMILY by **Patricia Davids**,
the next book in **THE AMISH BACHELORS** miniseries,
available in July 2018 from Love Inspired.

Paul Bowman leaned forward in his seat to get a good look at the farm as they drove up. Both the barn and the house were painted white and appeared in good condition. He made a quick mental appraisal of the equipment he saw, then jotted down numbers in a small notebook he kept in his pocket.

"What is she doing here?" The anger in his client Ralph's voice shocked Paul.

He followed Ralph's line of sight and spied an Amish woman sitting on a suitcase on the front porch of the house. She wore a simple pale blue dress with an apron of matching material and a black cape thrown back over her shoulders. Her wide-brimmed black traveling bonnet hid her hair. She looked hot, dusty and tired. She held a girl of about three or four on her lap. The child clung tightly to her mother. A boy a few years older leaned against the door behind her holding a large calico cat.

"Who is she?" Paul asked.

"That is my annoying cousin, Clara Fisher." Ralph opened his car door and got out. Paul did the same.

The woman glared at both men. "Why are there padlocks on the doors, Ralph? Eli never locked his home."

"They are there to keep unwanted visitors out. What are you doing here?" Ralph demanded.

"I live here. May I have the keys, please? My children and I are weary."

Ralph's eyebrows snapped together in a fierce frown. "What do you mean you live here?"

"What part did you fail to understand, Ralph? I… live…here," she said slowly.

Ralph's face darkened with anger. Paul had to turn away to keep from laughing.

She might look small, but she was clearly a woman to be reckoned with. She reminded him of an angry mama cat all fluffed up and spitting-mad. He rubbed a hand across his mouth to hide a grin. His movement caught her attention, and she pinned her deep blue gaze on him. "Who are you?"

He stopped smiling. "My name is Paul Bowman. I'm an auctioneer. Mr. Hobson has hired me to get this property ready for sale."

Don't miss
HIS NEW AMISH FAMILY by Patricia Davids,
available July 2018 wherever
Love Inspired® books and ebooks are sold.

www.LoveInspired.com